THE TEN-MILE TRIALS

*This is the latest in the acclaimed
Jake Hines detective series.*

When a dead man is discovered in a suburban house that is being used as a drugs lab, Captain Jake Hines pulls in all his detectives to investigate. The victim carried no identification but the discovery of a small Mass card written in a Cyrillic alphabet hidden in his jacket gives Jake an important lead - a ruthless Eastern European gang may have started operating in Minnesota. Meanwhile, a rash of burglaries are hitting the city and the way they are staged indicates that the perpetrators are new in town. Jake must work fast if he is going to track down the gang responsible, however, economic cutbacks are hitting the squad hard and the detectives have their work cut out for them.

*Elizabeth Gunn titles available from
Severn House Large Print*

The Jake Hines Series

McCAFFERTY'S NINE

The Sarah Burke Series

COOL IN TUCSON
NEW RIVER BLUES

THE TEN-MILE TRIALS

Elizabeth Gunn

Severn House Large Print
London & New York

This first large print edition published 2011
in Great Britain and the USA by
SEVERN HOUSE PUBLISHERS LTD of
9-15 High Street, Sutton, Surrey, SM1 1DF.
First world regular print edition published 2009 by
Severn House Publishers Ltd., London and New York.

British Library Cataloguing in Publication Data

Gunn, Elizabeth, 1927-
  The ten-mile trials.
  1. Hines, Jake (Fictitious character)--Fiction.
  2. Police--Minnesota--Fiction. 3. Detective and mystery
  stories. 4. Large type books.
  I. Title
  813.6-dc22

  ISBN-13: 978-0-7278-7922-6

Severn House Publishers support The Forest Stewardship
Council [FSC], the leading international forest certification
organisation. All our titles that are printed on Greenpeace-
approved FSC-certified paper carry the FSC logo.

Printed and bound in Great Britain by the
MPG Books Group, Bodmin, Cornwall.

ACKNOWLEDGMENTS

I am greatly indebted to Officer Quinton Gleason, his dog Sam, and the other officers and dogs of the Tucson K-9 Corps for letting me observe their training regimen.

In Minnesota, Officer James Bradley and Officer Mark Darnell introduced me to the close-knit band of brothers that is the K-9 Corps, and in Tucson, retired K-9 Officer Doug Russell also shared his insights into the rigors of training and caring for a police dog.

Sgt Mark Fuller, supervisor of the Tucson Special Investigations Division, Street Crime Interdiction Unit, provided colorful details about multi-tasking Russian gangs who occasionally invade the US drug trade. I rearranged some details to serve the needs of this story, but I'm not clever enough to have thought of wearing gold jewelry with velour running suits.

And without the generous help and ingenuity of John Sibley, retired Deputy Chief of the Rochester, Minnesota Police Department, the Ten-Mile Trials could never have taken place.

ONE

That Friday started out like most June mornings in Minnesota, somewhere between extra pleasant and perfect. The first cutting of hay across the road from my house showed a sparkle of dew as I drove by, and smelled like bee heaven. Red-winged blackbirds flaunted themselves in the ditches along the highway, and a meadowlark in a nearby pasture promised his mate great sex if she'd just come home. To confirm that all the planets were lined up right, somebody had made a fresh pot of coffee in the break room and I got to it ahead of most of my comrades in the Rutherford Police Department. I carried a cup to my desk feeling smugly content. Minnesota is usually quick to punish undue optimism, so the rest of that day may be partly my fault.

Shortly before lunch, a row of fleecy white cumulus clouds began building on the western horizon. Two hours later they'd become churning behemoths with a black layer on the bottom and thunder rumbling inside.

The first gust hit at two thirty, and within a few minutes a monster wind was blowing pieces of Rutherford up into the sky. Like some cosmic Cuisinart, the storm blended pitchforks and potato peelings, gable-ends and garbage cans into a lumpy flying mulch, which it spread across a wide swathe of southeast Minnesota halfway to Lake Pepin. Behind that path of destruction, tons of rain and hail dropped into Rutherford and its surrounding farms. By nightfall, Hampstead County was a hive of busy insurance adjusters.

Police officers going off shift rubbed their bruises and groaned with fatigue.

'Man, when I say I'm a beat cop today,' Bud Burnap said, 'I *really* mean beat.'

'Tell me about it. I pulled at least a dozen people out of flooded cars this afternoon,' Vince Greeley said, 'and they all yelled at me like it was my fault.'

'There was this one woman,' Bud said, 'on top of her car with two little kids. I can't imagine how she ever got them up there. I said, "Lady, couldn't you see this was a river?" And she said, "It's my driveway, for cat's sake." – like that should make the water go away.'

I'm the captain in charge of the investigative division, and have plenty of worries of my own. I don't usually waste time in the break room listening to belly-aching patrolmen, but I was hoping one of them could tell me the driest route to my babysitter's house.

'Fifteenth and Marvin? The near Northwest is kind of tricky, it's got some low spots,' Bud said. 'If I was you, I'd go out Center Street all the way to the highway and come back in around the Costco store.'

'No, listen, you can just take Third Street and go straight out,' Vince said. 'That's good all the way to Fourteenth Avenue for sure. And if you have to, you could walk from there.'

'He can't walk through water carrying a baby! Are you crazy?' Bud said.

'He won't have to. Almost all the sidewalks in that part of town are high and dry.'

'Oh, and almost is good enough for you? You sound like that lady in the driveway.'

I left them there arguing, which is their favorite off-duty sport. Bud and Vince have been friends since grade school, and most of their conversations seem to be stuck at about the ten-year-old level.

My Ford pickup has plenty of clearance, so I got it out of the lot and drove toward Maxine's house, improvising the route, telling myself I should have known better than to ask two street cops the best way to anything.

9

Driving as much as they do, they all get preferred routes to everything, and defend them like they were holy writ.

The rain had slowed down to an occasional sprinkle, but the streets were full of trash and tree limbs. I drove carefully, trying to peer around corners, alert for low spots. There was a stoplight lying in a tangle of hissing wire in the intersection at Seventh Street, and one homeowner in the next block had four dog dishes lined up on the top step of his porch, with a hand-lettered sign behind them saying, 'Take if yours.'

Oddly enough, the beginning of this big storm had caught me unawares, because when it started I was hunkered over the desk in the chief's office, locked in mortal combat over the budget.

'No use yelling at me about it, Jake,' McCafferty said. 'The city council's in a panic, I've never seen them so lathered up. They say the tax base is eroding out from under them, the next six months are a crisis. The mayor read a letter from the power company that says if the city can't stay current with their bills they'll cut us off.'

'They wouldn't, would they?'

'He thinks so. He says get ready, by Thanksgiving we're all going to be wearing long underwear and keeping the thermostat

10

set low. Speaking of freezing, they froze their own salaries, so you know they're serious.'

'That may prove they're serious, but it won't save enough money, will it? What are they quoting for the deficit?'

'Five million and growing as we speak. We must find ways, they say, to get along with less. Prioritize your needs, maximize the assets you have.'

'If I maximize the assets I have any more than I'm doing now, you can go ahead and burn the chairs for heat, because nobody will have time to sit down.'

'I know. But it's no use arguing, Jake, the money's not there. Twenty per cent cuts across the board they're demanding, from every department. Demanding, not asking. Non-negotiable.'

'Well it can't come out of investigative staff,' I said, 'unless they want people to start writing up their own incident reports.'

When he didn't answer I looked up, found his eyes looking through me at some distant planet, and realized he was considering what I'd just said.

'Come on,' I said, 'that's a joke.'

'Maybe not.' He had his head cocked a little, like a robin looking at a worm. 'We've already put the phone on automatic. If people can listen to all those other options

11

and select by number, maybe they could punch one more number and get a form that lets them answer the first half-dozen questions we always ask.'

'Please, Frank, tell me you're kidding.'

'I mean, what are they? Name, address, phone, fax, email. Right?'

'Well, right. And with a little work, maybe we can train them to go right on to the number of victims and the condition of the bodies! What else?'

'I never said it would work for homicide. But for a lot of property crimes, all those stolen bikes and missing wallets, we could have an express line like that. It would speed things up when we call them back, so that— What?'

'You're really not going to let me add the two detectives I've been begging for all spring, are you?'

'Haven't you heard a word I said? There is no add for anybody this year, there is only subtract. You can go ahead and bring Amy Nguyen on board to replace Darrell Betts, since that's already in the pipeline. But we don't get to replace Bo Dooley, and the new video-recording equipment for the interview rooms is on hold.'

I reminded him that Rutherford's population had ballooned above a hundred thousand in the last year, and the crime rate was going up, not down.

'It always goes up in hard times,' Frank said. 'Nothing I can do about that, either.'

'Can't we just keep the same cars another year?'

'That was one of the cost-cutting measures we initiated in January, remember? We've only bought three patrol cars this year. Every Sunday at Mass now I say an extra five Hail Marys for the continued good health of our fleet mechanics and the warranty service at Paulson Motors.' He banged a few folders into a precise pile on his desk, taking out his frustration on the paper goods. 'We've got to put a total freeze on overtime, and Property Crimes has to shed two people by the end of the fiscal year. You and Kevin figure it out. Prioritize, Jake. Maximize your assets.' He stopped talking and stared over my shoulder. 'Why is all that stuff flying around?'

I turned in time to see an aluminum lawn chair sail past his window, followed closely by an open umbrella and a wastebasket. Frank McCafferty's office is on the second floor, so the view from there does not ordinarily include household items. We watched in rapt silence as two towels and a striped sock followed the other chattels aloft. Then thunder shook the building and wind-driven rain

13

hit the window like bullets. A ragged piece of awning flew by, and phones rang all over the building.

I got up and trotted toward my office, where my phone, of course, was ringing. Three detectives called in quick succession to tell me why they were calling off the field work they had planned for the afternoon.

'You think I can't see out the windows?' I asked Ray Bailey, who was questioning a suspect in a mobile home park. 'Quit talking and get in here before that tin can you're sitting in blows away.'

By the time I got a chance to call Maxine's house, the hall outside my door was full of breathless people who'd just come in out of the weather and were standing around dripping and telling each other how bad it was.

Maxine answered in the standard day-care provider's voice, quick and quiet, trying to shoehorn a short conversation into her life before she was interrupted by the urgent demands of a preschooler. Maxine's clientele doesn't like to be kept waiting. Call her in the daytime, you want to state your business briskly, in short words.

I asked her, 'Everybody still got feet on the ground over there?'

'Oh, Jake – yeah, we're OK. Something's

banging, though. Hold on.' There was more banging, and then footsteps and she was back. 'That storm door on the back has a tricky latch.'

'I hope my family is still there with you?'

'Ben's sleeping, and Trudy just went out. Wait, here she is back.'

Trudy came on and said, 'Wow, did I get my mind changed in a hurry!' She laughed, not very merrily. 'I got almost to the car and realized I wouldn't dare open the door for fear the wind would blow it off.'

'Don't even think about going out. Big pieces of the city are flying through the air. Are you going to be all right over there? Do you need any help?'

'Wait, I'll ask Maxine.' She said something away from the phone and got a quiet reply, came back on and said, 'She says we're fine.'

'Good.' Then I didn't want to let her go, so I said, 'Sorry about your afternoon jaunt. You got out this morning, though, didn't you?'

'Twice, actually. And he was fine both times.' She had been spending days at Maxine's house this week, going out often for shopping and coffee dates so the baby would get used to being left. As far as I could tell from the times she'd left him with me, Ben wasn't picky about his companions as long

15

as he got enough to eat. Trudy was the one having anxiety fits. 'Tell me to quit being a wuss and just go back to work.'

'OK. Quit being a wuss and just go back to work.'

'Easy for you to say. What do fathers know?' Her three-month maternity leave was ending. Intellectually, she was itching to get back to her job as a forensic DNA specialist at the Bureau of Criminal Apprehension in Saint Paul. She knew she was lucky to have the best day-care provider in town, my own former foster mother, Maxine Daly. But leaving the baby she'd devoted all her time to since the day he was born was turning out to be much harder than she'd expected, and she was sharing every bit of the pain with me so I wouldn't feel left out. 'If I get any more conflicted about it, I'll break in two,' she said. 'What if it turns out I can't do it?'

'Please don't worry about that. If you can't go back to work we'll just declare bank-ruptcy and move out of our house into a homeless shelter.'

'That's it? That's the comfort you offer your suffering spouse?'

'I can only give you what I've got.' Unfor-tunately, what I had was perilously close to nothing. We had remodeled our mortgaged-to-the-max house before we could afford to,

16

using mostly barter and sweat equity, and then had a baby sooner than we intended. We were in hock up to our eyebrows.

But I couldn't stay worried about it because we had this great place in the country with big trees and acres of land, halfway between our two jobs, and now we had Benjamin Franklin Hines, a child I privately judged to be the champ of this year's baby crop. He was learning to wave his fists and kick in triumphant greeting when I leaned over his crib, sometimes actually getting both eyes focused on me and giving me gummy drooling almost-smiles that told me I was a prince of a dad. Every time Benny looked at me like that, I congratulated myself for having been clever enough to assume all this debt before the credit crunch shut off the money spigot. Let other people worry about abstractions like the market. I was sitting pretty with everything I wanted.

Picking my way around broken glass and somebody's mailbox, I negotiated the soggy corner into Marvin Street and parked in front of Maxine's house, relieved to see that her front gate was still there and not sagging much more than usual. Most of her shingles seemed to be still in place, and I couldn't see any broken windows. To my surprise, Maxine's foster son Eddy Payson was squatting in the crotch of the oak tree in her front yard, on the platform I'd built for him there. It wasn't quite a tree house yet, but I had plans for it to grow into one, and a couple of steps and handholds built on the trunk. Nelly Dooley was up there with him. She smiled and said 'Hi, Jake' when I got out of the truck.

'Hey,' I said. 'Aren't you kids a little damp up there?' It was a rhetorical question. Their clothes were soaked and their hair was plastered to their scalps by the rainwater still dripping off the leaves.

'Kinda,' Eddy said. 'But this is the best place to watch all the police cars on the corner. What are they doing, Jake?'

'I don't know. I just got here.' I turned to look where he pointed, and saw the flashing light bar on an RPD patrol car, turning into the street at the other end of the block. It wheeled into line with three other black-and-whites already parked there. The newcomer had a K-9 cage in back. As I watched, Darrell Betts got out of the driver's seat, walked around to the back gate, and began to unload his dog.

'Oh, boy,' Eddy said, 'look at the dog!'

Watching a K-9 dog makes you feel you have been going to work every day with the wrong attitude. I've always said I was proud

18

and happy to be a Rutherford policeman, but next to a K-9 dog I look like a surly foot-dragging slacker. So enraptured about going to work that he can hardly contain his joy, he whines, he yips, he paces his cage. Every muscle in his body seems to be saying 'Let's go do it!'. He doesn't have to be urged into action by his trainer – from the moment he gets loaded into the vehicle at the beginning of his shift, his brain is focused like a laser on one glorious thought: he is an Alpha dog on his way to another big win.

But I was familiar with the edgy electric aura a K-9 dog brings to a scene – what held my attention now was the change in Darrell. I'd heard he was happy about his move to the K-9 unit. Now I saw that working with the dog was turning Darrell into an Alpha man.

Not that he was craven before, or ever failed to hold up his end – he had always been solid as a rock. A little bit like a rock in every way, in fact. Kind of dense, if you want the truth.

He was on my crew until a few months ago, not my hire but part of the squad when I joined it and still there when I made lieu-tenant. He'd come on board about the same time as the incandescent Rosie Doyle, and because of her I didn't notice him much at first. There were very few female police officers in Rutherford at that time; and Rosie, red-haired and voluble, was the first to make the rank of detective. Some of the guys had grave doubts about her qualifications, but the chief was impressed by her work record and test scores and admonished us all to play nice.

'Yeah, keep your PC face on while she gets you killed,' Andy Pitman muttered. He was a big, ugly patrolman, with a stellar reputation on patrol in the toughest parts of town. Nobody could say Andy Pitman ever ducked a fight, but his great specialty had always been defusing hot spots so everybody went home with the teeth they came with. A flat-foot cop of the old school, he thought putting women on the police force was a ridiculous idea and promoting one to the homicide squad was going out of your way to court disaster.

Among her many other achievements, Rosie turned out to be the investigator who proved Andy Pitman wrong. Intelligent and hard-working, cheerful and energetic, she wore down everybody's resistance. All the men of her family were in law enforcement, and she had done five years on street patrol without a whimper. So she was preconditioned to know what to expect, when to go all in and when to be careful, and even when to shut up, although that was always the hard part for her.

Darrell seemed slow and stolid compared to the quicksilver Rosie. In fact, relative to the rest of that crew of detectives, Darrell sometimes came across as the clinker in the heap. A big-shouldered weightlifter who often spoke English as if it was his second language, he became famous on the crew for statements like 'I told him he was skating on pretty thin water here'. The other detectives on the people crimes crew liked Darrell a lot, though, and in time I came to value the solid virtues that his quirks had camouflaged. He was tireless and patient, he never complained, and he always did what was asked as well as he possibly could.

Watching him now, I saw that he moved with new assurance and spoke to his animal in a voice that had taken on a new timbre of authority. He had added body armor under his uniform blouse, as all the K-9 officers did because they worked the most hazardous situations, usually at night. The added bulk made Darrell's chest and shoulders more impressive than ever – he looked as strong and solid as a tree.

Why in the world, though, was he unloading his dog on Maxine's street? She lived in a marginal neighborhood of older one-family bungalows, admittedly the kind that often slide into deeper poverty and dysfunction. But Maxine's block had always been filled with hard workers like her who kept it peaceful, partly by never having much in sight to steal or envy.

Fighting my instincts, I called Dispatch. The new Dad in me wanted to skip the information, grab my wife and child, and beat it out of there. I stuck with procedure because I'm a cop; I cared about Maxine and all the other kids in her house, and knowing always beats not knowing.

Dispatch said the problem evidently started at the height of the storm, when two men ran out of the house on the corner, jumped in a car at the curb, and drove away in the rain. A third man came running out after them, yelling. A big gust of wind caught the storm door just as he opened it, and blew it off its hinges. The yelling man, holding on to the doorknob, was pulled out with it and dumped on his face in the driveway. A neighbor, watching the storm out his window, called 911 to report a householder in trouble.

The first responder was Anton Hruska, a one-time Preston High wrestling champ with a crooked nose, always called Ruskie by his fellow cops. He fought his way out of his vehicle in the wind, helped the man out from under his house door, and led him staggering back into his house. Once inside the incredibly messy living room, Ruskie saw at once that a bloody nose and the cost of repairing the door were going to be the very least of this skinny fellow's problems.

Hruska called for backup, hard to get right then. One patrolman came over from the east side as fast as he could. It must be bad, Dispatch said, because the second officer requested help from Domestic Violence and then, a bit later, a K-9 team. Beyond that, she said she didn't know anything yet – but wasn't that enough?

As I closed my phone, a cop I didn't know came out of the house leading the skinny young man, still damp, in ragged jeans and a sleeveless T-shirt. He had a wispy goatee, a long, thin pony tail, and elaborately tattooed arms and hands, which right now were handcuffed behind his back. Behind him, Bo Dooley led a pale, sobbing woman in dirty cut-offs and flip-flops, with a wet towel pressed to her bloody face.

'Oh, look,' Nelly said, behind me in the tree. 'There's Daddy!'

'He's working,' I said. 'He won't be able to talk to you.'

'Well, I know *that*,' she said, insulted.

'Excuse me,' I said. 'Of course you do.'

It was mind-bending to see my one-time icy-eyed vice cop at his new assignment in Domestic Violence. His appearance had always walked some interesting line between flaky and elegant, carefully calculated to blend into any bar scene or rave. Usually, Bo wore diamond earrings and a neatly trimmed beard, often with spit-shined Western boots and an ancient, cracked leather jacket. Now he was clean-shaven and wore a neatly pressed cotton shirt and slacks. Otherwise, he seemed to be the same Bo he'd always been, poised and tightly wound, fully in command of his situation.

Last out of the house was a county agent that I recognized from the Department of Social Services. She had the hardest job, carrying a terrified child who was literally kicking and screaming. 'Help me, Mommy!' the little girl yelled, to the woman Bo was loading into his car. The mother turned toward her child, crying, but Bo put his hand on the woman's head, pressed her firmly into his squad, locked all the doors, and drove away.

When she was gone, the child's hysteria escalated. Beating on her rescuer, she tried to wriggle free, and went on screaming till she was belted in and carted away. It was hard to watch, but too riveting to turn away from. Uneasy about the two kids behind me on their observation platform, I looked up and recognized with a shock their stoical, matter-of-fact expressions. That's how it goes, their small faces said.

I myself was once one of those waifs and strays that Maxine takes care of, a ward of the State of Minnesota from the day I was found in a Dumpster, a wailing infant nobody wanted. Besides not knowing who I was, nobody ever figured out what race I belonged to, since I had indeterminate brown skin and a face that looked as if it was composed of spare parts from several continents.

It came back to me now how readily I accepted the suffering of others when I was Nelly's age. I've been lucky enough to build a happy life for myself as an adult, and I guess it must have softened me up a little – I hated watching that little girl get dragged away. I bet Bo Dooley, right now, was wishing he was back on my crew.

Maxine, seeing me standing in her driveway, opened the door of her house and asked, 'What's going on?'

I told her what I'd just seen and she said, 'I hate to wish anybody bad luck, but really I'll be glad if those people are gone for good.'

'Have they been giving you trouble?' I was surprised by her comment. Maxine's been around some tight corners herself in her day and it's made her compassionate – she hardly ever criticizes anybody.

'They've never said a word to me, but they're sure not anybody's dream neighbors. Noisy fights, and people coming and going at all hours.'

'Dopers, you think?'

'Who knows? Sometimes they seem to sleep all day, but when they're awake I feel like I have to keep an eye on my kids when they're out in the yard. I've been really hoping they'd move.'

'Well, it looks like you got your wish.' I watched the third car peel off and disappear. 'Did you know they had a child in there?'

'Yeah.' She gave me an uneasy look. 'I know what you're thinking, I should have reported it. But you know, around here' – she shrugged – 'nobody's got much, and we all try to mind our own business. Who's got time to fight?'

'I know.' I didn't have any time to spare either. I needed to help Trudy get Ben home before he got hungry. I went inside and began packing up and hauling out some of the elaborate gear required by my son for a day away from home. For one infant who could not sit up yet, it was really quite an amazing array. Fatherhood had intensified my interior debate about whether to hang on to my gas-guzzling pickup. The more things Ben needed, the more I wanted to keep the truck and the less I could afford it.

I packed Trudy's car and put the overflow in my truck. Trudy strapped Ben into his car seat while she repeated, for the hundredth time, all the instructions for Ben's first Monday alone with Maxine. When our expressions told her that she absolutely must not go over it one more time, she got into her car and headed for home.

Maxine's other day-care kids were being retrieved by their moms by then, and they both wanted to hear about what was going on at the end of the block. In the middle of all that talk Eddy and Nelly got bored with watching police cars, climbed down out of the tree, and came indoors. Nelly went in and lined up her dolls for a tea party, but Eddy, who had just turned eight, had begun to take an interest in cooking. Right this minute he had decided he should make fried potatoes for supper. As soon as he could get Maxine to listen, he began to tell her precisely how he planned to go about it. She was pretty dubious about letting him stand

27

on a stool to fry potatoes in hot oil; but he said he was 'absolutely positive' he could do it without burning himself.

She settled him at the sink with four potatoes and a paring knife. 'If you can peel all four of them without bleeding,' she said, 'then we'll talk about the frying.'

She followed me outside to say goodbye. On the step she blew hair out of her eyes and said, 'Remember how hard I tried to get that kid to talk when he first came here?'

'Yeah. I was just thinking, I kind of miss that speechless little stalker who used to hug my leg until I sat down and let him climb on my lap.'

Eddy was one of Maxine's most impressive successes. Three years ago, he'd been a silent wraith scared out of his wits by his father's insane destruction of their whole family. For a long time, after his social worker dropped him off here he would point or nod at what he wanted, but never talk. The first few words Eddy spoke brought tears to Maxine's eyes. He had had some tough days and nights in the years since, but with counseling and therapy he had mustered the nerve to go back to school. Now he'd finished second grade, was reading a little, and lately, to everyone's surprise, had begun to show an amazing gift of the gab.

I hugged her and told her she was my hero. 'Your hero is thinking about getting some earplugs,' she said. 'But it is good to see him bloom.'

As I turned to get into my truck, I saw that still more RPD vehicles had parked at the end of the block. Al Hanenburger must have driven one of them – he was out on the street now, walking from house to house, telling the several householders standing on their front steps that they would be wise to wait inside for a while.

He walked up to Maxine's step and said, 'Excuse me, Ma'am, you live here?' Then seeing me, 'Oh, hi, Jake.'

'Hey, Al. What's happening?'

Hanenburger told us, 'We've got a problem with that house down the street there. You probably want to stay inside,' he told Maxine, 'till we get this situation squared away here.'

Eddy was in the doorway now, asking Maxine, 'Do I have to take out all those eye thingies?' I told Maxine, as she turned to go in, 'I'll go see what's up, and be right back.'

Walking back to the corner, Al told me, 'The two people they took out of the house say they live here. They were using – there's meth and pipes on the table. But because of how it started, two guys yelling and running

29

out, Ruskie asked if anybody else was in the house. The guy said no, just me and my old lady and her kid. But while they waited for the woman to get dressed, Ruskie went out in the kitchen and asked her through the bedroom door if there was anybody else in the house. She said somebody – some name he couldn't understand – might still be out in the garage, she wasn't sure. Ruskie said, "He live here too?" And she said, "Over my dead body. That guy's crazy." So Ruskie went back and asked the tattooed man, "What about the crazy guy in the garage?" He shook his head and said, "Don't listen to my old lady. She's been tweakin', she don't even know what day it is." Something about how he said it convinced Ruskie he was lying, so he phoned in for a search warrant to be faxed to him, and while he was at it he asked for more backup and a K-9 unit.'

Al gave a little grunt of laughter. 'Everybody but me was already out on an emergency, so Ruskie's gonna have to manage with just me and the dog.'

'Hey,' I said, 'that should be plenty.'

'Probably,' Al said, 'if the dog can shoot.'

He was being unduly modest. Al Hanenburger got his spot on the Emergency Response Unit crew by being the best shot in the department.

I stood with Al and Ruskie, watching Darrell walk his dog across the front of the house. The dog was all business now, sniffing the air in a wide herring-bone pattern that grew narrower as he approached the attached garage on the far side of the house. As he reached the cement apron in front of the garage, the animal went noisily berserk. He flung himself at the big overhead door, scratching and barking at the top of his lungs. He was one big, bad, dangerous dog, he wanted us all to understand, and as soon as Darrell let him off the leash he was going to tear open the garage and eat its contents. I believed him – he seemed very sincere.

After a minute Darrell was apparently satisfied that he understood the message, and began telling his dog that was enough for now. He got him to switch gears by tossing him a white ball with a little leash of its own. They played tug-the-ball for a minute while he told this big snarling beast what a very good dog he was. It seemed a strikingly inaccurate description of the dog's behavior, but it matched the dog's opinion of himself, and the killer canine morphed into a romping pet before our eyes. Darrell rubbed the big hairy head and scratched the upstanding ears while he slathered the dog with extravagant praise, and then said 'Sitz!'

– which turned out to be German for sit (the unit's puppies were raised in Germany and the Czech Republic). I was fascinated to see that Darrell, who had never quite mastered English, seemed to have no trouble with German commands.

Sitting didn't appeal at all to the explosively energetic dog, but he managed it after a few seconds with just a little protesting butt-wiggle. Darrell spoke a quiet word to Ruskie and Al, walked up close to the garage door, and said loudly, 'Whoever's in there, we know you're there and we're giving you a chance to come out with your hands up and empty. If you don't come out I'm going to send my dog in after you, and he *will* bite you. So you better use your head now, and come on out.'

He was answered by an implacable silence.

'OK,' Darrell said, to the other two officers, 'I'm ready to send in the dog.'

'Uh ... hold up one minute, will you?' Al said. 'ERU just got a new gadget that might be just the thing for a situation like this and I'd like to try it.' He walked across the street to where his car was parked, opened the trunk and took something out. It looked like one of those dinky dumbbells people carry for arm exercise when they walk, except this dumbbell was black and had wheels front and back.

He walked quickly across the street and up the driveway to the garage that had set off the dog. Choosing a metal bar from among the many implements dangling from his belt, with one quick and brutal gesture he broke the small side window of the garage. He tossed his dark little device in through the broken window and trotted back to his car.

'You want to see how this gizmo works, Jake?' he asked me. 'It's called a Recon Scout. It's a robot.'

He pulled another device out of his crammed-full trunk and turned it on. It was the receiver for the little electronic spy he had dropped into the garage. As we watched the screen, he tried the joystick. The robot backed up a foot. He gave a little grunt of satisfaction. 'There we go. How about that?'

I asked him, 'How'd you get it to land on its wheels?'

'It's got a ... uh ... widget that keeps it right side up.' We watched as his device pivoted away from the window. He hit a switch and the gadget grew night vision, an eerie green glow. 'Oh, wait, though,' Al said. 'I don't need this, do I? Hoo-ee! Lights all over the...' Then we both, said 'Aah!'

Maxine's noisy neighbors had a grow house in the garage.

TWO

Darrell told his dog to stay where he was, and walked over to see what we were looking at. He watched while the image scrolled across the crowded scene in the garage – leafy plants growing thickly out of identical plastic tubs, upward toward the big mercury-vapor lamps hung from the rafters.

'Jesus,' Darrell said, 'it looks like the forest crime-evil!'

'The what?' Al's face got the puzzled look so common to people talking to Darrell. Then he went back to watching the monitor, smiling with satisfaction. My olfactory nerves had begun to twitch, in anticipation of the syrupy smell waiting for us in the garage.

'Boy, Darrell, give your pooch there a couple of extra treats for me,' Al said. 'He sure called this one right.'

'Well, good.' Darrell was watching the monitor curiously. 'Where is he?'

'Who?'

34

'What?' They were staring at each other, hurling monosyllables back and forth like an Abbott and Costello routine run amok.

'Darrell,' I said, 'all we can see in there is a grow house. Why'd you think your dog thought he'd found a person?'

'Because all Sam goes after is people. He hasn't done his drug-detection package yet.'

'Trained or not, he found us a grow house this time,' Al said. 'Look at the monitor.'

'I don't care what the monitor shows,' Darrell said, 'and neither does Sam. He wouldn't know weed from my Aunt Fanny's fanny. What he does know is how to find a person when I say to do it. He's really good at it, too.' He looked at Al Hanenburger, standing there so proud of his electronic toy, and back to where his dog still sat anxiously in the driveway, grumbling in his throat. 'If I was you,' he said, 'I'd call for some more backup. Sam thinks there's somebody in that garage, and I never seen him be wrong.'

Al Hanenburger gave him a long, agonized stare and went back to watching the monitor. 'There's nobody moving around,' he said. 'I don't see anybody in there.'

'I don't either,' Darrell said.

'But you still think—'

'Yup.'

Slowly, with every move betraying his

35

reluctance, Al Hanenburger plucked his phone off his belt, dialed his duty sergeant, and initiated a complex conversation. He thought they might need backup to go after the human being the dog insisted was in the garage. But he also figured they'd need a drug-interdiction unit to deal with the marijuana plants. 'And there was meth and paraphernalia in the kitchen, so does that mean I have to wait for those folks too before we go in?' He listened a minute and said, . All we can see in the garage is a forest of hemp.' He asked Ruskie, 'Any sign of a meth lab in the house?'

'Not in the two rooms I saw.'

Hanenburger repeated that into the phone and listened a minute, squinting in concentration. As soon as the voice paused, he said, 'Well, but whoever's in the garage is probably not friendly, would you guess? He ain't gonna stand around and watch while a lab crew cleans up the— I'm not being smart, I'm just saying— Look, Sarge, the robot shows a grow house, that's all we can see. But Darrell's dog says...' He listened again, then raised his head and asked Darrell, 'Dead or alive?'

'Sam don't care,' Darrell said, 'long as he gets to bite somebody.'

Hanenburger relayed that information,

listened a minute longer, and said, 'Gotcha.' He put the phone back in its holder. 'Sarge says it might be quite a while before an ERU can get here. He's saying, if your dog is ready to go in there and get the guy, we should back you up while he does that. So what do you say?'

'I say fine. You guys ready?' Everybody nodded. 'Let's do it then.' Darrell looked around. 'Let's see ... Al's the best shot, let's put him here in the middle. Ruskie, you stand over there on the left, and—' he looked at me. He was pumped, enjoying being in charge of the scene. 'Whaddya say, Jake, I guess this next part is a little below your pay grade, huh?'

'Except when you're short-handed like this,' I said. I'm not given to undue heroics, but I wasn't going to go sit in Maxine's house while Darrell's little band of brothers went after the bad guy in the garage.

'OK. Please don't shoot my dog.' He was not on my crew any longer, so he could afford that little swipe that he'd probably been saving up for years. Walking back to Sam, he took off the dog's leash and said 'Fass!'

Sam got up at once, delighted, and resumed his fang-and-claw behavior, barking madly and scratching at the bottom of the garage door. Darrell walked over to the old Dodge Dart at the east edge of the driveway, opened the driver's-side door, and touched the electronic doorlifter fixed to the visor. Al and Ruskie and I stood braced on the cement apron, with our weapons aimed at the middle of the rear wall. I half expected a volley of lead to pour out as the door slid up. Instead, we faced a short forest of leafy green herbs where nothing moved.

Sam went through the plastic tubs in three leaps, a tawny brown streak of power, knocking plants right and left. When he reached the cupboard against the back wall, he began pawing and snarling at the bottom of the tall central doors.

'One last chance,' Darrell yelled. 'Come out right now with your hands over your head or my dog will bring you out.'

Nobody answered. 'Hold your fire, now,' Darrell said softly. He ran along the west inside wall of the garage, cut sharply in to the front of the cupboard, and pulled the middle door open. Snarling, Sam leaped on the body lying on the bottom shelf and dragged it out, climbed on top of it, and sank his teeth in its upper arm.

Darrell had to use all his new expertise then, shouting *'Fooey!'* as he quickly handed Sam the white ball. Sam didn't really want to quit biting the man, since biting the man was the *FCber*-reward that his macho life was aimed at. But he was, as Darrell repeatedly reminded him now, a *good* dog, a *very good* dog, a *very, very good* dog. He seemed to understand the English for that just fine. And as Darrell petted Sam's big wolfish head and crooned to him about his superior qualities, he let himself be led away, chewing and tugging on his white ball and drooling with glee.

In the grateful silence that followed his departure, we cautiously approached the body, which lay motionless where Sam had abandoned it, on the garage floor. I bent and touched the artery behind its ear. It was still a little warmer than the floor, but no pulse beat there. I stepped back to look at the whole length of the corpse. A man, I thought, though so battered and bloody it was hard to be sure. His injuries from Sam amounted to no more than a couple of punctures in the shoulder of his jacket and drool marks down the front, but he had been beaten severely and shot many times before he died. There was a dark stain of urine between his legs. All of his clothing, from neck to toe, was streaked and spattered with blood, and he and the cupboard reeked of it.

The three of us stood around the grossly

abused body, waiting for our ears to quit ringing and our heartbeats to slow down a little. Then we all did what men of action do in the twenty-first century. We each pulled a cell phone out of its holster and dialed a number.

I called Ray Bailey, head of my People Crimes section, gave him the address on Marvin, and told him I was looking at a body.

'New or old?'

'Just died, I think,' I said. 'He's in a grow house in a two-car garage. He was badly beaten before he died, and the person who shot him conveniently left the murder weapon beside him in the cupboard.'

'Jeez, they're killing each other over a roomful of buds now?' Ray's the kind of guy who can make a silence feel sad. After a few woeful seconds, he vented his Friday night sigh. 'OK, I'm on it.'

I asked if he needed any help rounding up detectives. 'Five thirty on a Friday,' I said, 'they might be kind of scattered.'

'I know most of their hangouts,' he said. 'But OK, you want to help, how about you call the BCA and the coroner for me? I'll get one of my guys over there to inventory the dope and get it moved to the storehouse.'

I caught the coroner just as he walked into

his house. He wasted no time on elaborate greetings, just said 'Allo?', listened to my story, said 'Yah, OK,' and hung up in my ear. Adrian Pokornoskovic, whose Ukrainian name was so hard to pronounce that we all called him Pokey, had survived extreme cold and near-starvation in a work camp behind the Iron Curtain before he was grown. His small stature, in fact, was partly the result of many missed meals in adolescence. Those years had made him dubious of all authority and tough as nails – he never complained, as the rest of us did, if we spent all night standing in a snowbank or slogging through cold rain.

Another man his age who had worked all day on his feet might express regret about being called out on a Friday night to examine a corpse. But Pokey loved forensics and gladly abandoned the zits and wrinkles of his dermatology practice whenever we called him to come to work for us. Hampstead County still got by with a part-time coroner, since part-time in Pokey's case implied no lack of due diligence – he waded into a crime scene as if it was a privilege to be there, digging through stinking dirt and the detritus of sordid violence, looking for the truth.

The BCA call was smoother and more bureaucratic, a matter of waiting through several rings, poking the right numbers after the tape answered, and getting grilled for specifics before placing the name of our department in the queue at the request desk. The Bureau of Criminal Apprehension was becoming a huge system. Crews dispatched from its gleaming new building in Saint Paul in effect added the Bureau's top-of-the-line scientists and equipment on to our smaller force. Trudy reminded me often that Rutherford crime got service every bit as good as big metropolitan skulduggery.

'We have the best of everything now. We *are* the best. Other states send their mitochondrial DNA work to us. Doesn't that make you proud?' That was on one of her cheeriest days last month, when the pains of childbirth were forgotten, Ben's schedule was smoothing out nicely, and return to work was still a distant, alluring dream.

Now when she answered my call I could feel the heat of her insecurities come blasting across the radio waves. She had just pulled into the yard at home, Ben was awake and fussing, and she needed to get inside and warm a bottle. That was the other big adjustment going on, the switch to bottle feeding – she had taken pills to dry up her milk, and she had to add formula prep time to the many other routines that were fighting for primacy in her brain. The switch from Earth Mother to Techno Mama was giving my lover a bumpy ride.

I told her what was going on and why I hadn't left town yet. 'I wanted to see this situation stabilized before I left Maxine,' I said, leaving out any mention of my native curiosity.

'OK. Come as soon as you can, though, will you? I've got a carload of gear and groceries to get inside.'

'Leave all the stuff in the car,' I said, 'I'll get it when I get home.'

'Which will be when?'

I was beginning to understand how Eddy felt about his potatoes. 'Half an hour,' I said. 'Soon as my People Crimes crew gets here, I'll be out of here in two minutes.'

I walked past Ruskie's car to let him know that Ray's crew was on its way. I could hear him as I walked toward him, reading his systematic way through the search warrant worksheet he held in his hand. The stilted language made him sound as artificial as a long-range weather forecast. 'Judge Tolliver? This is Officer Hruska of the Rutherford Police Department. Will you swear me in please?' He told the judge about the grow house they had inadvertently found in the garage, and about the paraphernalia in the

43

kitchen. For these reasons, he said, he needed a warrant to search the rest of the house and the grounds around it, as well as the rest of the cupboard in the garage and 'two other cabinets on an adjoining wall.' As attorneys get smarter about fending off the results of searches, police warrants become more and more precisely detailed – it's an arms race both sides urgently want to win.

When he finished, I told him about the two crews that would shortly join him here. I left him stringing crime scene tape with Al Hanenburger, and hurried back to Maxine's house to let her know her street would soon be swarming with law-enforcement types of every rank and color.

'I'm afraid you'll be living on a very busy street for a couple of days,' I said. 'But hey, you'll be in the safest place in town – crawling with cops.'

'That's true, isn't it? Plus it gives Eddy a lot to watch.'

He had even more to watch before sundown. I was forty miles away, unloading Trudy's car, when Ray called and said, 'This damn house is turning out to be like the creature that ate Detroit.'

'What now?'

'Ruskie got his search warrant OK'd by the judge just before I got here,' Ray said. 'Nobody else was here yet and there wasn't anything to do for the stiff till the coroner saw him, so Ruskie and Al and me, we decided to go ahead and look through the house.'

The ground floor was just the stinking mess you expect with drug freaks, he said. 'We found a little more meth in a kitchen cabinet, along with some pot that smelled like the good stuff in the garage. But it looked to us like the little girl had been sleeping on a sleeping bag on the kitchen floor, and the parents were using this dinky bedroom – probably meant to be a den – off the living room. So Ruskie says, "Wonder what they got against the upstairs?" and we went up. The smell got stronger and stronger as we climbed the stairs. By the time we opened the door at the top we were already guessing what it was. They been setting up the mother of all meth labs up there, Jake.'

Four rooms full of top-of-the-line gear, Ray said. 'No messy little pissant camp stoves here – a big propane cooker. Supplies stacked against the walls. You hear what I'm saying? Almost a superlab.'

'Ray, listen, you don't want to touch any of that stuff.'

'You think I'm crazy? I closed the door and we all went back downstairs while I called the county Health Department. The person

45

who answered the phone got all huffy about it being after hours and Friday night – like I should have had the good sense to find it Thursday morning. So I got huffy back, about this mess being in the middle of a crime scene in a residential neighborhood, and we yelled at each other for a while till I told the young lady if I don't get an ETA for a clean-up crew within half an hour I'm calling the director.'

'But now it's been half an hour and you can't remember who that is,' I said.

'And if I could, I don't suppose he'd be exactly bowled over by a call from a city police detective, do you think? So will you call him?'

'Sure. Tell me first what number you called before, so I can start there.'

'You think?'

'Damn straight,' I said. 'I'll stay on it till I find the right person – we have to get that crap out of there, you guys cannot work around that, and neither can ... Oh. Damn.'...'

'You already called BCA, I bet,' Ray said.

'Yeah. We weren't exactly next in line, but ... I better call them back. Talk to you later, Ray.'

I'm not much of a politician, but over the years you get to know some people. So after

46

the number Ray gave me played a tape saying the office was closed, I called my old buddy Ivan. He's a Health Department scientist I play poker with occasionally, and what I happened to know about him is that he's the kind of good husband and hard-working plodder who goes home and cuts the grass on Friday nights. I caught him there and explained my plight. He got back to me in a few minutes to say, with an embarrassed laugh, that a clean-up crew was already on its way to Marvin Street. The woman Ray had the fight with dispatched them as soon as she cooled down, but though she had noted down the correct address she got too steamed up to make a note of Ray's number and was trying to reach him at home, where Dispatch thought he was.

'I don't know why Myra went off on your guy like that, Jake,' Ivan said, 'except everybody's uptight because they're overworked and afraid of more job cuts.'

'Tell me about it,' I said. 'I've never known Ray to get crosswise of anybody that way before. But we're taking a beating too – seems like we lose someone every week. Thanks, Ivan, I owe you a big one.'

I told Ray his crew was coming, skipping most of the details about crossed signals because he still had the whole damn night to work. 'What about the body?' I asked him. 'You find any ID on him?'

'Not a scrap. No records, no money, no watch. Surprised they left his shoestrings. I told Pokey he'd better get good fingerprints, they're all we got.'

'Pokey's there?'

'Come and gone. Soon as I told him about the mess upstairs, he came right away with the meat wagon and grabbed his corpse. He said no use letting the Department of Health decide it was toxic waste, it wasn't anywhere near the meth operation and he wanted his crack at it first. So I had Andy take a bunch of pictures and he rolled it away. When I didn't say anything, he said, "What? You think I shouldn't have let him have it?"'

'It's Pokey's call, I guess. For all we know, the guy was just there to buy some pot. Let's not pick a fight with the coroner, we don't have time. Is your crew all there?'

'Yeah. Rosie's in the garage getting all herbed up, taking samples. Andy's in here shooting really dismal pictures, and Winnie and Clint are outside looking for trace evidence. They found eight casings in the garage. Nothing outside but grass, so far. What does BCA say?'

'We're to call them and reinstate the order,

48

as soon as the Health Department says the place is clean.'

'After which, there won't be anything left here worth the trip from Saint Paul.'

'Good point. So we better hope for stellar performances from Pokey and my smart wife, who is going to go back to work on Monday and will probably have to win this ball game for us.'

Trudy had put the baby to bed and was standing across from me at the island in the kitchen, peering into some of the sacks I'd brought in. She pulled a couple of used formula bottles out of one of the sacks and frowned at them. Ben, in the next room, let out the first whimpers of a baby getting ready to cry. Store-bought meals didn't suit his digestion as well as the ones he'd been getting from Mama, so he often cried as much after meals as before them, behavior guaranteed to make new parents pull out their hair.

I told Ray, 'Talk to you later,' and folded up the phone. Watching my wife carefully, I said, 'I learned a new word since I saw you in town.'

'Oh?' She was rereading the label on the formula can.

'Yes, I think it's magic. Watch my lips.' I pushed out my jaw and sternly said '*Sitz!*'

49

'*Gesundheit!*' She stared at me, eyebrows forming a question.

'That's funny,' I said. 'Every time Darrell says that, his dog sits down.'

'Ah,' she said. 'So that's what you were doing at the crazy house. Watching Darrell and his K-9 dog.'

'Yes.' Ben gave an exploratory wail, the first high note that warned of many more to come. 'I really do want you to sit. Will you please? In the rocker, right here.' I moved it closer to the island. 'Then I'll bring the big guy out—'

'Jake, there's so much to do...'

'No, there isn't. It's Friday night. There's really only one thing to do, which is for you to hold Ben till he falls asleep, and me to unload the rest of the gear and cook dinner while I tell you about my day. Doesn't that sound cozy?'

'For sure,' she said. 'You do have such cozy days.' She liked it, though – it was what she wanted to do. Ben burrowed his hot un-happy head into the hollow above her collar-bone and bitched about the rotten luck that had brought him this bellyache. After a few minutes of protest, he brought forth the big belch that eased his pain. When he quit squirming and fell asleep, I started some burgers on the grill outside and reminded

Trudy that the great thing about ceasing to be the family milk fountain was that it meant a lady could have a glass of wine before dinner.

'Hey, yeah. Ooh, insane, bring it on,' Trudy said, and put Ben back in his crib. I broke out the bottle of Shiraz I'd been saving for this occasion, and we toasted her return to the land of grown-ups. Over dinner, I finally did share some details about the bizarre scene at the other end of the block from Maxine's house.

'So much crime in one house, incredible.' She sipped and thought. 'That couple ... the few times I noticed them, they just looked like a pair of losers.'

'Didn't they? I'm not very surprised about the grow house, but I'd never have guessed them for a big-time meth lab. What Ray's describing – that takes capital. And they certainly didn't look like cold-blooded killers.'

'No. Maybe hot-headed grudge-holders, though.' She shivered. 'I hate the thought of leaving Ben in the same town as all of that, much less the same block.'

'You know any babysitters living in mansions? And grow houses get found in some very nice neighborhoods these days.' She knew I was right about that. Real-estate markets were churning, and good houses were

51

available for rent. And if they can, growers rent in quiet residential neighborhoods, which are the best cover for a cannabis crop.

The meth lab was something else. Crystal meth hit Minnesota hard in the nineties, and by the turn of the century its users were swamping law-enforcement budgets in small towns, pouring into the court systems and crowding the prisons. The drug quickly took hold in rural areas and small towns because it was cheap and could be manufactured out of readily available chemicals – in country kitchens and even the trunks of cars. Hey, just follow the recipes on the Internet, the kids told each other gleefully, and you can buy the cold remedies in any drugstore. And the rush? Oh baby, sick, sick.

It flooded the brain with dopamine and enhanced sexual pleasure, so it appealed especially to the young, and was so powerfully addictive that just a few samples could hook people for life. The dependency was devilishly hard to break, and the effects catastrophic – it gave people hallucinations, rotted their teeth, and aged pretty young girls into crones with devastating speed. And they didn't care. A good hit of meth, they assured the appalled health-care providers trying to rescue them, felt like ten of the best orgasms you ever had, all at once. Narcs are not people who are easily disgusted, but I have seen a meth lab and its clientele turn seasoned officers somber and pale.

The Minnesota legislature, spurred on by their alarmed constituencies, passed laws requiring cold remedies based on ephedrine and pseudoephedrine to be kept behind the counter, sold one to a customer, and signed for by the holder of a bona fide ID. When the kids got smart and started fanning out to buy cold remedies in all the small towns around, they passed another law that drugstore chains had to keep system-wide records and check them often. The penalties for infractions were big fines and prison terms.

The new laws worked well for a while – discoveries of meth labs in Minnesota dropped like a stone in the next couple of years. The self-congratulatory tone of the news stories surrounding that achievement were quickly muted by a second discovery, close on the heels of the first: ma-and-pa meth labs were disappearing, but addicts were not. All states don't pass identical laws, and the United States has long borders and open shores. We had pushed meth manufacture out of the hands of amateurs and secured the trade for the pros. So for the last year, when the narcs brought in speed freaks with stumps for teeth, shaking with tremors and screaming with paranoid delusions, the query *du jour* became 'Where's all this stuff coming from?'

'It's got to be Mexico,' Frank kept saying. 'Why can't Border Patrol do its damn job?'

Now I'd stumbled on a new twist.

'This is starting to feel like the perfect storm,' I told Trudy that Friday night. 'The same day I get word we're facing budget cuts and a shrinking staff, I find out one of the places the meth is coming from is down the street from my babysitter's house.'

THREE

After dinner Ray Bailey phoned to say he had just secured the crime scene. 'I sent my guys home,' he said. 'The clean-up crew is here, and the good news is it looks like this meth lab was just being set up. These geeks in the plastic jammies say it's never been used, the gear is clean. They have to take everything out in a certain order, though, and a lot of it is volatile material. We're lucky and the neighbors are very lucky, this could have been much worse.'

'So, you're just turning the keys over to the clean-up crew—'

'And Rosie. The DOH guys won't let us touch anything on the property till they certify it clean – but they said since none of the seals on the supplies were broken, she could stay by their van and inventory it as they bring it out. Equipment too, they're letting her make a complete list of brand names, shipping tags, and so on. We should be able to trace a lot of this back to the sellers and put the squeeze on them for purchase orders.'

'Good! How soon do you get back in?'

'I asked them to call me when they're getting ready to leave. They said don't hold your breath, it's a big job, but maybe some time tomorrow'

'OK.' I cleared my throat. 'About tomorrow—'

'Yeah, Pokey's autopsy. I was going to call you about that in a minute.'

'I bet he's hell-bent to do it right away, isn't he?'

'Oh, sure, you know how he is. It's on for ten o'clock at Med Sci. I'd like to send Clint, he hasn't done one in a while; but his kid's got Little League, he's going to groan.'

'Which is nothing compared to the noise Frank's going to make. He spent two hours this morning getting his bowels in an uproar about the budget. No overtime, was one of his new rules – ironclad, he said.'

'What are we supposed to do, though? I have to send somebody—'

'What I was wondering,' I said, 'was if maybe you could attend the autopsy? Then I'd run in to town tomorrow morning, find a judge at home, and get your two new prisoners bound over till Monday. Maybe I'll drop by the crime-scene house and check on

56

that, and I'll check on the prisoners. The rest of the work could wait till Monday. What do you think?'

'This is how you propose to handle the shortfall? Work the execs harder to eliminate overtime?'

'Well, from now on we'll put our foot down with Pokey, no autopsies on the weekend. I just thought maybe on this one case, while all the brass is having shit fits about the budget, you and I might cover it and pile up some credit for an emergency.'

'You're expecting something worse than five felonies in one small dwelling?'

'Well...'

'Looking for maybe a drug war and a nuclear attack on the same day?'

'Never mind, Ray. It was just an idea.'

'OK.'

'OK what?'

'OK, I'll do it.'

'You're sure? It's not too much on top of—'

'If you promise to hang up right now and not talk to me any more tonight, I'll attend the autopsy.'

'Thanks, Ray. I really do appreciate—' I did hang up then, because I was talking to a dead phone.

Clearly, Ray Bailey was going through

some kind of a bad patch. He'd never conformed to my image of a cheerleader, but it wasn't like him to be this grumpy, either. I made up my mind to find out about it as soon as time allowed, which was a prospect too distant to worry about on a Friday night.

I did some work in the garden early Saturday morning, got on the phone, and found out which judges were on call. I was sitting in the kitchen having the second breakfast that rewards extraordinary virtue when the phone rang and Pokey said, 'Hey, Jake, that pretty girl lives in your house, she close to phone?'

'Yes she is, I'm happy to say. Her name is Mrs Hines now. You remember that?' She was pouring me another cup of coffee and I handed her the phone

'Hey, Pokey,' she said, smiling, and I could hear his voice warm up on the other end. Trudy and Pokey have a mutual admiration thing going. 'Yeah, I'm going back Monday. Oh, the baby's no problem, Maxine's holding a place for him. Everybody's ready but me. Hmmm? Well, for one thing, all my clothes are too tight.' It was true. She'd put on weight, or anyway girth, carrying Ben, and for the first time since I'd known her she was wailing about having nothing in the closet to wear. Her mother was helping her move buttons and ease seams, since our clothing budget, never lavish, now totaled zero. It was one more anxiety in an already overloaded week.

Pokey managed one soothing cluck over her clothing problems and plowed right ahead with his own concerns. I heard the word 'autopsy,' and then I thought I heard the word 'history'. But why would he talk to Trudy about that? Whatever he said seemed to take her mind off her overstretched seams, anyway. Her face smoothed out and then grew a little frown of concentration as she listened. She said 'Mmmm' and 'Uh-huh' and 'Oh?', and then 'Well, no, you know how forensic DNA analysis works, we all have to look at the same thirteen loci, thirteen areas of junk DNA that don't code for any proteins or ... No. Well, money and time – plus privacy concerns. Take your pick, they all end up at the rule saying we don't go nosing around, we just look in those thirteen places.'

'If you had the funding,' she continued, 'you could maybe take it to one of those labs doing family trees ... Hmmm? No, I never ... My Mom already has more family than she knows what to do with.' She chuckled, listened some more, and said, 'Or find a lab full of genetic scientists who are looking for anomalies ... Hmmm? I guess it could cost a bundle. Tell you what, I could ask the guys at work if anybody knows some postdocs with a grant doing studies in...' She finished the sentence with an impenetrable thicket of what I call 'Black Ops code,' the science jargon she shares with Pokey and her lab crew at BCA. As far as I'm concerned, it might as well be Urdu.

But whatever it was, it cheered her up. She hung up and said, 'Really, that Pokey's brain is a wonder, isn't it? The things he notices...'

'What's he noticing today?'

'It's that John Doe you just sent him. Most docs would just say oh well, a drifter and a druggie, who cares? But Pokey sees a lesion and starts spinning out a theory...' She hummed a little tune while she fed Ben and put him in another layer of clothes. She had me carry his portable crib out to a sunny patch in the garden, put him in it, and let him practice grabbing at the dangling toys while she hoed the corn.

With so many new chores to manage for the baby, we had agreed to raise only half as much garden as the last two summers. That meant we were fifty per cent short of the produce we'd been growing to pay off our debt to the Sullivan brothers for remodeling our house. Trudy had managed the complex barter by which that loan was restructured, stretching out the remainder of the debt over two more years, extending their rights to the use of my fishing boat and our ten acres of hayfield across the road, and keeping me enslaved to their hay crop twice every summer for years to come.

It was lucky that Ben was a very superior child, so I never begrudged what he cost me. I did remind my mate occasionally that fishing was fun and haying was donkey work, and any reasonable accounting would show that the Sullivans were getting paid well above top dollar.

'Sweetheart,' she said, 'if you don't like the bargain I made you're welcome to ask the bank for more money.'

'Come on, you know there isn't a chance in hell—'

'Exactly. So put a sock in it.' We had been through some version of this conversation several times and there was no need to repeat it this morning. The hay was not quite dry enough to put up and I had a job to do in town.

Minnesota law gives us forty-eight hours, no more, to hold a prisoner before he goes to court for his initial appearance before a judge. While this supports the important

61

principle that justice delayed is justice denied, it could also lead to an understandable reluctance to arrest anybody on Friday. But there's wiggle room, in the form of a waiver, built into the law. So the first thing I did when I got to town that morning was hustle up to the Judge Sorenson's house and get his signature on a document saying we could hold the Marvin Street miscreants over till Monday.

I then went down to the jail to check on the prisoners, and was enchanted to learn that the underfed and overdecorated male half of this team of lawbreakers was named Hogarth Peter Weber. Clearly, his mama had expected a larger life for her boy. I found him taking his ease in the messier end of a double cell, his flamboyant arms partly covered by the jail's orange jumpsuit.

I asked him, 'Your friends call you Hogarth?'

'My friends call me Pete,' he said. 'But you don't need to call me anything until after I've seen a lawyer.'

'You called him yet? Because you'll be seeing the judge on Monday.'

'And when I do, I'll ask for a court-appointed lawyer.' He knew the drill very well.

'You're claiming you're broke? All that meth and pot in your house, that was free?'

'None of it's mine except that little bit in the kitchen that the old lady was sucking on. That took my last dollar, that and the milk and cereal for her kid. Women and kids,' he said, shaking his head sadly, 'they'll bleed you dry every time.'

'Your story's so touching, Hogarth. But maybe you should be thinking about doing some good for yourself while you wait.'

'And I could do that how?'

'Easy. Cooperate with us now. Tell us all about the men who ran out of your house in the storm. Were they going to help you market the weed you were growing in your garage?' He smiled at me blandly and said nothing. 'Tell me all about that and make nice with the judge on Monday, you might earn a chance to plead down from Murder One on that dead body in your garage.'

'There's a dead man?' I watched his face while he realized I hadn't said it was a man, and that he'd just confirmed he knew all about the stiff in the garage. His eyes grew slightly more opaque, and a tiny sneer formed on his upper lip. He held on to his crazy arrogance, though, determined not to be knocked off balance by a little mistake. 'I'm sure sorry to hear about that. The Brooklyn Dodgers must've had a little argument.' He shook his head sadly and clucked.

I knew right then that when Ray asked him about it later in court he would deny he ever said 'dead man'.

'The Brooklyn Dodgers? That's what you call your suppliers? Where can we find them?'

He wagged his right index finger. 'After I get me a lawyer, you can ask him what he wants me to talk about.'

One good thing about an unrepentant sleazebag like Hogarth Peter Weber, he saves you time. You can see right away that he has grown a thick, impermeable shell, and the hollow space inside where his feelings should be is filled with smart-ass attitude and layers of greed and sloth. From that first conversation, I knew that Hogarth Peter was not going to cooperate in anything but his own defense. He would fight to the last ditch on the county's dime, and would finally go to prison anyway on at least some of the wide array of charges he was facing. He'd live a long time there at public expense and his every effort inside would be directed toward getting drugs and alcohol and sex, the only things left that interested his shriveled mind. He had become a costly waste of skin, and I walked away from him quickly when I realized I was fantasizing about turning Sam loose on him.

I went over to the women's side of the jail to find Gloria Funk in the infirmary. She had been weeping and distraught when I'd seen her being led out of her house, and though she'd had some repair work done on her battered face – she was wearing a pressure bandage over the top of her nose and another on a cut on her cheek – she seemed even more strung out than she had been at the house. Besides withdrawal pains, her jailers told me, she was suffering from extreme anxiety about her little girl. Watching her sniffling in her bed, I thought how many questions about the dead man in the garage could be cleared up quickly by Gloria Funk, if she had enough sense to seize the day. So I walked to the end of the corridor and called Ray Bailey's cell phone.

He answered from what seemed to be a cavernous space, faint echoes of his voice bouncing back at me from cold steel and tile. I said, 'You're still in the autopsy room? What's up with that body that it's taking so long?'

'Well, five or six bullet holes, and another wound track that he hasn't decided about yet. Plus nobody can find any match on his fingerprints. Pokey's having a wonderful day, working on a nonperson full of holes.'

I told him where I was and described the

difference between the two prisoners.

'Weber's never going to give us anything he doesn't have to, but the woman seems to be very anxious about her little girl. I thought she might ID the body and tell us what went on there and why they killed him, in exchange for a chance to see her kid. What do you think? OK if I ask her a couple of questions?'

'Oh, hell, yes,' he said. 'No use getting all technical about the lines of authority now. Way things are going this year, you and I might end up cleaning the toilets.'

I wanted to suggest that we not complain about the taste of cat food until we were actually eating it, but he had already given me the concession I wanted, so I let it go and walked back to Gloria Funk. She was in a ward with three other women, who were getting very sick of listening to her cry.

'God, get her out of here, will you?' the thin freckled one said. 'She's driving everybody up the wall.'

'Because nobody will *tell* me anything,' Gloria wailed, clutching at me, trying to grab my hand. 'I don't even know where my daughter is. Can't you at least tell me that?'

'She's being taken care of temporarily by Child and Family Services,' I said, 'and she can be transferred to your mother's custody as soon as your mother is ready to take her. Gloria, would you like to come upstairs and visit with me a while?'

'Oh, sure, visit,' the freckled woman said, perversely switching sides now that I was trying to do what she'd asked. 'Don't tell him *nothing*, honey.'

But Gloria still had some speed in her system; she desperately wanted to talk to somebody, and I was there. I put a robe and handcuffs on her and we walked up to the visitor's lounge, where I cuffed her to the table leg and sat down across from her. I borrowed a family-size box of tissues from the attendant's desk, because her nose and eyes were running water like hillside springs. I believe she was the dampest woman I have ever interviewed, and I have talked to some world-class weepers.

But the lounge didn't work for her; she kept peering nervously over her shoulders. 'Gloria,' I said, 'there's no recording equipment in here, this is just a visiting room for families.'

'Sure, but how do I know who's listening?'

Her alarm seemed genuine and I was afraid she might change her mind about talking to me, so I called a guard to bring her upstairs to an interview room in the investigative section.

'Now,' I said, once we were locked inside the small soundproof room, 'you don't need to worry about being overheard in here.' I tried to make light of the fact that this conversation would be recorded, as the law requires. After I read her the Miranda warning, I said the date and our names and told her, 'We're being recorded for your protection as much as mine, so you can be sure I won't do or say anything inappropriate.' The stiff formality sounded so ridiculous, spoken to this forlorn woman in these grim surroundings, that I sat still for a few seconds, uncertain how to proceed. What the hell would be an appropriate thing to say to a woman with a meth habit and a beaten face? I wished I had somebody to monitor the interview on the outside, but there was nobody around on a Saturday and I decided the DVD would be enough.

I've watched that conversation several times since that day, and it always confirms that my judgment was correct. That recording is more than enough, I believe, to make anybody watching it think twice about the pleasure of vice in general and meth in particular. I still find it hard to watch. It isn't every day you get a glimpse of the way lighthearted folly can lead to genuine soul-sucking despair.

She was sick with shame, that's what it came down to, and rightly so. She would remember for the rest of her life, she said, and I believed her, the way her four-year-old girl had reached out to her in terror, begging to be allowed to stay with her mother. She remembered every one of the child's pleas and repeated them to me, word for word, until I almost begged her to stop.

'And I couldn't do anything,' she wailed, as her nose grew redder and her eyes swelled shut. 'People were holding on to me and holding on to her, and what could I do? I was helpless.' And the terrible thing, she wanted to make sure I understood, was that her child had always trusted her completely. 'I mean I know you think I'm a terrible person because you found me in that house with all the dope and everything – but I mean, listen, I always took care of my baby, she knew she could count on me.' And she meant it, too, this heedless young woman who had 'kind of run with the wild crowd,' she admitted, in high school, but dropped out and got a job when she found herself pregnant. She'd had to fight to keep the baby because everybody kept reminding her she had no means of support. 'And they were right about that part. Boy, flipping burgers just doesn't cut it once you've got a kid.'

But against all the evidence, she saw herself as a reliable parent, a rock that her child could cling to. 'I mean I wasn't going to give away my own baby. Duh, what kind of a lowlife would do that? Besides, nobody gets all shocked any more if you're not married, and I knew I could manage some way. I was like, hey, babies are fun! And she was, my Tiffany, she's always been a smiley little charmer, all my boy friends have loved her.'

Her mother had helped her at first, but Gloria lost her counter job at McDonald's for wisecracking and making too many mistakes, and then got fired from Kmart for hiding out in the stock room with the cute boy with the pricing gun. 'But really you have to do something at those places, they're *so* boring.' After she lost the second job, though, her mother said it was time for some tough love. She put their clothes out on the porch in two plastic sacks and changed the locks on the house.

'And then for a while,' she said, trying for a light-hearted shrug that looked incongruous with her battered face, 'we lived here and there, with friends.' Till Pete, one sunny day last October, found her in the park where he was idly toking up and she and Tiffany were feeding bread to the geese. They shared a nice, giggly afternoon, and he took them home with him. Not to the house on Marvin Street – Pete lived in a small apartment then.

'Was he dealing from there?'

'Just a little pot, enough to keep us in smokes and make enough on the side for, you know, food and stuff.' She made a little gesture that waved away the seriousness of food and stuff, then chewed her lip silently for a few seconds and finally said, reluctantly, 'And he arranged for me to turn a few tricks to keep us going when we were short.'

Early in the spring, though, he met some guys in a bar and came home and told her they were 'moving up'. Three months ago, give or take, they had moved into the house on Marvin Street. 'And business, like, picked up.' Big, dangerous-looking men brought bags of weed and started Pete on his delivery route. They set up the grow operation in the garage, taught Gloria how to tend the plants, and began bringing gear and supplies for the meth lab on the second floor. Gloria believed Pete had been making pretty good money since then, but she couldn't be sure. He gave her what she needed to buy groceries and run the house, but never a regular cut. Once, when she tried to have a conversation about money, Pete got very angry, called her a cunt, and shoved her around, so she never had the nerve to ask again.

Lately, Gloria said, she had been 'rethinking her relationship' with Pete. (She actually said it just that way.) Pete had stopped being any fun at all a while back, and they'd had to give up their sleeping quarters on the second floor of the house because the men needed it for 'producing product'. Well, from then on they had to live all crowded together on the first floor.

The men who brought the supplies and took away the money were creepy and threatening. They talked funny and got mad when she didn't understand what they said. 'They helped themselves to anything in the refrigerator, too. Never even asked. And they were so weird – the way they wore those plastic gloves all the time and yet smelled terrible, left their filthy socks and underwear all over the place, and changed clothes wherever they happened to be standing. Pete said if I didn't want to see it, I could leave.'

She could see Pete was afraid of them too but didn't want to admit it, and more and more he took his fear and uncertainty out on her and Tiffi.

She began looking around, considering her options. 'But,' she said, with a quick sideways glance at me, 'by then I'd started using a little meth, see, and that made it tougher to think about making a change.'

I knew this would be the hard part, talking about how much of what she had been using. Bo always said you should take whatever amount people admitted to and double it. I'd been careful not to press her about anything, hoping that talking would calm her down. When I asked questions she answered them willingly, but mostly I let her drift along, telling her story at her own speed. But now that we'd come to the story of her burgeoning meth habit, she became defensive and agitated, first insisting she wasn't really hooked and could quit any time, then scuttling sideways toward her fear that she could not quit, it was already too late for that.

'I mean every day I feel like I don't need it at all until just when I get to the point when I *do* need it. Then I think, just this one time more. While things are so stirred up and crazy, I think I better have a little snort to steady my nerves.' She uttered a wild peal of laughter and said, 'I hope that's perfectly clear.' Then she clutched her hair, said 'Oh, God', and collapsed onto her own arms on the little desk between us, weeping uncontrollably again. 'I mean you just don't know,' she blubbered. 'Until you've tried it, you have no idea how fast it takes over everything.'

Now that, I thought, sounds like a true

statement of fact. So while she seemed to be completely unnerved, with all her pretenses put aside for the moment, I leaned over her heaving shoulders and said, 'OK, Gloria. You came up here saying you wanted some help finding your daughter, and now you seem to be saying you need some help fighting your habit. I can hook you up with people who'll help you with both those problems, as soon as you tell me the name of the dead man in the garage and explain how you and Pete came to kill him.'

She sat up wild-eyed, tears still streaming off her face, her mouth a round O of shock and terror. 'Dead man, what dead man? We never – oh no, no, please no, what are you saying? Look, I know you think ... I know we shouldn't have got involved with those guys, it's not right to sell meth and shit, but – there's a body? Please, Sergeant – oh, or is it Lieutenant?'

'Captain,' I said. 'Jake Hines. You're saying you didn't know there was a homicide at your house?' She nodded vigorously with tears flying off her face – yes, that's what she was saying. And the nutty part was I more than half believed her. 'But how could you not know?'

'The storm?' she said helpfully. 'It made a lot of noise. And then ... they were all in the garage and I was in the kitchen. Besides' – she looked miserable again and suddenly, like a piece of bad meat that's impossible to digest, a morsel of unpalatable truth popped out – 'I was tweaking. My stupid brain wasn't working right. Oh, God.' Then she whirled on her little stool and faced the wall. Her shoulders heaved and she said again and again, 'Oh, God. Oh, God, what have I done to my baby? Oh, God!'

I stood up and said, 'I think maybe we've talked enough for one day.' I couldn't stay in that little room any longer, listening to her describe with devastating accuracy how much abject misery she had caused herself and her child. Let her dry out until Monday, I thought. And a sneaky corner of my brain added that then it would be Ray's job to listen to her.

But maybe one more thing... 'What was his name?' I asked her. 'The dead guy.'

She grabbed a handful of tissues out of the box and mopped her face as she whirled back to face me. 'I have no idea. I could never tell them apart and I couldn't understand their names and I don't know why any of them would kill any of the others except they always seemed ready to, any minute.'

'How many of these guys were there?'

'Four, I think. Or maybe five. I told you, I

75

can't tell them apart.'

'Always the same ones?'

'I think so. They were so big and ugly and loud, I tried not to look at them, but ... yeah, I think it was usually the same three at the house, two older and one young, and sometimes a fourth one that seemed like the boss.'

'Which one hit you?'

'Oh, that was Pete. They were making so much noise, they woke Tiffany up from her nap. So I yelled at him, told him to make everybody shut up, and he knocked me across the room.' She touched the bandage on her cheek, tentatively. 'Those guys scared him and he always tried to act tougher when they were around.'

'What were they fighting about that day?'

'Oh, who knows?' She made a frivolous gesture, throwing up her hands and rolling her eyes. That stupid gesture made me suddenly furious – she'd held me in this steamy little room, listening to her ranting sobs, and now she couldn't be bothered to take my questions seriously. I stood up and pulled out my keys, thinking I would send her back to her bed in the infirmary. By tomorrow she'd be in a cell and I would be at home in the country, where I could forget about her miserable wasted life.

She had her face all dried off but when she

saw me getting ready to leave, her eyes brimmed over and a fresh stream poured down her face. 'Oh, no, please. Listen ... please. I'm trying to think.' She reached out toward me, with a wet tissue still balled in her hands. 'They were in the kitchen, the two biggest guys, mean and with the funny names. Yelling at Pete about the orders, always yelling. He called them the Brooklyn Dodgers, but I called them the Screamers.'

'Why did he call them that?'

'Oh, they claimed to be from Brooklyn, to have a whole big family there.' She made that waving away gesture again, the one that had made me so angry. This time I realized it was her default gesture to dismiss anything she couldn't understand, to try to make it seem ridiculous. 'Maybe they were in Brooklyn before they were here,' she said, 'but you only had to hear them once to know they were ... foreigners.' She pronounced it 'for'ners', and her upper lip grew a little sneer.

'OK, so they were screaming about the orders. What about them?'

'I think they were saying the money wasn't right for the last deliveries, it should have been more. And Pete said don't yell at me, talk to— What did he call that younger one?

Sair ... something. He was out in the garage, the young one, packing the weed in that picnic hamper he always carried. The rest of them were all in the kitchen arguing. Pete said, 'I always make him' – he meant that Sair guy – 'shake hands when I hand over the money, and Gloria here takes our picture so I can show you he agreed it was all there. Show him the picture from this week, baby, go on.' I said I can't look for any picture with my nose bleeding like this, and he said you better find it right now if you don't want some more of the same. So I went and found the stupid picture he'd just maneuvered that youngest thug into posing for. The picture had nothing to do with the money, just some contest Pete convinced him they were going to enter. He's always so *clever*, you know, always working his little scams on everybody. But I didn't say anything, believe me. I did not want to get in the middle between those yahoos one more time.

'The two older Screamers looked at the picture, Pete and the young Screamer with their thumbs up, all smiles. After they looked at the picture, the older guys swore and went out to the garage.

'The wind had started blowing really hard a few minutes before. Tiffany was still crying because they woke her up and she was hungry, and I didn't have anything in the house to feed her. I told her to wait till the wind stopped and I'd go get her something. That made her cry even harder, and Pete said make her shut up and went out into the garage. So then I couldn't stand any of it a minute longer – so yes, I admit, I went in the other room and had another hit off the bong. So OK, there's some time there that's kind of vague. Very, very vague, actually. They were all arguing in the garage but the noise kind of blended in, I couldn't tell how much was Screamers screaming and how much was Tiffany crying, and then there was storm noise on top of everything. There was a big roll of thunder and then two of them ran in from the garage and out the front door. They slammed it all shut behind them, the inside door and the storm door, but Pete came right behind them, he was yelling too, something about you're not gonna leave that mess here for me to clean up. He pulled the inside door open and left it open and when he turned the handle on the outside door it went flying, the door and him with it, wind blowing everything all over the house.

'Tiffany ran to me, terrified, and jumped into my arms. I carried her into the bathroom, I always heard that's the safest place to be in a wind storm. I put a wet towel on

79

my face and closed the door. We sat in the tub and I sang to her. Then I heard all these other people come stomping in ... Was there a dog?'

'Yes.'

'I thought maybe I dreamed that part. Then they took my baby away.'

She started to puddle up again but the thought of the dead body in the garage had settled her down some, she knew her life was at stake now. She held her hands up, palms toward me, saying, 'Wait, I'll stop crying, I promise.' She made some hiccuping noises, and after a few seconds she took a deep breath and started over.

'Here's what I have to say. I admit I like my pot in the evening and now I'm about half-way to being a meth freak, but I can beat both of those. I know I can, if you'll get me some help. I absolutely know I can do that and get my baby back and take care of her. The other thing I *absolutely* know is that I never killed anybody. I did not do that, no, that is not something I would do.

'So will you...?' She looked up at me quite matter-of-factly for a few seconds, as if she was asking to borrow a cup of sugar. Then the magnitude of the trouble she was in seemed to sink in a little deeper. She swallowed a couple of times, took another deep breath, and said hoarsely 'Please help me!' Her throat dried up completely then, and her last word came out in a terrified squeak, 'Please?'

FOUR

'God!' Kevin Evjan said Monday morning, 'I had such a good weekend I can hardly raise my arms.' He flopped into the spare chair in front of my desk, stretched out his long legs until the whole front of my office looked done over in gray flannel, and sighed happily.

Kevin is a winning swimmer in the world's gene pool – his Norwegian father passed along broad shoulders and a noble chin, and his Irish mother added bright-blue eyes and a dazzling smile. Not surprisingly, his good looks are only exceeded by his high self-esteem. I would not be able to tolerate him in the same building with me except that his exceptional energy and cockiness allow him to manage the dismal slog that is Property Crimes, year in and year out, without throwing himself in front of a bus.

His smug self-regard now enabled him to go right on describing his days off, despite my obvious lack of interest. 'Somebody told

82

me the slab crappies were really biting on Little Boy Lake, up by Longville. So I took a personal day Friday and put the arm on my cousin Henry. Henry's got a cabin up there, you know – well, you don't know, but trust me, it's a nice snug little place.'

I couldn't seem to turn him off, but I found his story so far from riveting that my brain had started to run through the powers of two ... 2, 4, 8, 16, 32, 64, 128 ... Math games get me through boring patches, though I usually quit the powers of two around 4096, when it starts to be more work than fun.

'But I didn't want the whole three days to be just about fathead minnows and sunburn, you know?' Kevin stretched again, luxuriously. 'So I persuaded that black-eyed girl from Victims' Services – Francesca, you know her? Yeah, the one with the—' He made a gesture that made me wish my door was closed. 'I talked her into coming along.' He chuckled. 'Fran-CHESS-ka ... Truly, as Hemingway would say, Italian names are just designed to turn guys on, aren't they?'

'Ray and I caught a homicide and worked both days,' I said.

'Too bad.' He didn't even slow down. 'You should grab some time up there, Jake, it's beautiful. Pack up Trudy and the baby and spend a couple of days on the water. Do you both a world of good.'

'Uh-huh. You bring home plenty of crappies?'

'Well ... some.' The self-satisfied smirk broadened on his handsome face, where I was beginning to dream of planting a lemon chiffon pie. 'Actually, we never got a line wet till the second day.' He chuckled again. 'Watch out for that Francesca, she's a fox.'

'I will. And I'm glad you had fun, because now you're going to have to bust ass for a while.'

'Oh?' He recrossed his legs and settled the crease in his pants. 'What's up?'

'The chief announced budget cuts on Friday. Twenty percent across the board, every section, no exceptions. Ray doesn't get to replace Bo Dooley, I don't get my new recording system, and you have to cut two detectives by the fifth of July.'

'The fifth of— Jake, that's the week after next.'

'I know.'

'Well, come on, that's ridiculous! I've already scheduled the next two months, it's too late to— Why do you keep shaking your head?'

'How long have you been gone? Are there no TV sets in Northern Minnesota? Surely

84

you're aware that we're in the midst of the worst financial crisis since the Great Depression?' I was beginning to sound like Frank McCafferty and it felt pretty good. I can manage the gravitas when I need to, I thought, and went on to my next punishing news. 'Also, have you talked to your weekend crew chief yet? They had another rash of break-ins on the far Northwest side. Phones ringing off the hook all day yesterday, and it's worse this morning. A lot of gold jewelry, coin collections, electronics ... small stuff with high value. Sounds kind of targeted. Better get on it.'

'Fine.' He stood up. 'You're a bundle of fun on Monday mornings, aren't you?'

'Yup. Bring me your revised schedule by close of business today.'

He sat back down. 'You're serious.' I nodded. 'Frank really means it?'

'Because the City Council really means it. The tax base is in the toilet, and they're having bad dreams about the power company turning off the heat in December.'

He stared out my tiny window. 'I don't see how we're going to...'

'Yes, you do. We might have to put a brave face on this for the public, but let's not bullshit each other. We're barely staying afloat now – I've been begging for more resources since last fall. Take away twenty percent and there are some calls you'll never get answered. Starting today, we're going to quit having weekly meetings. LeeAnn's setting up an in-house email site, and the three of us – you and I and Ray – are going to publish any changes to rules and regs, useful sources, late-breaking news, and helpful hints. And everybody's got to read it every day.'

'A house organ! My God, isn't that original? What are you going to call it, Uncle Jake's journal?'

'Go fuck yourself! This is not a joke, can't you get that through your head? After you've thought about who gets dumped back down to patrol, you and Ray and I – if there's time – will have one last meeting and prioritize.'

'Oh, now there's something to look forward to, a prioritizing session with Ray Bailey.' He beetled his brows, screwed his mouth down at the corners, and growled, 'Laptops and trail bikes can wait, goddammit, but we can't let a stiff lie around till we get to him.' His imitation of Ray's voice was pretty fair, I thought, but he could not twist his self-satisfied face to within a country mile of the legendary Bailey gloom.

'Go easy on Ray,' I said. 'He caught a real pisser of a case Friday night. I helped him all I could, but he's been working nonstop both

86

days. Something else is bothering him, too, but I haven't figured out what it is.'

'Oh, well, I can clear that up for you.' He glanced into the hall to be sure nobody was coming, leaned across the desk and hissed, 'The poor old dork's in love!'

'In love? Ray Bailey? With...' I puckered. 'Whom?'

'Oh, my gracious, *whom*? And from whence, you want that too? Whence is right down the road in Mantorville, and whom is that dowdy little waitress who was keeping house for the long-haul driver. The one you found shot and half-naked in a snowbank a couple of years back. Remember? The body under the overpass, and his eighteen-wheeler in two other places?'

'You serious? That woman who was so devastated? What was her name? Cathy something. Was it Niemeyer?'

'Yes. Doesn't it figure? The saddest woman you'd ever met, you told me.'

'Well, Ray and I were both impressed by how much she cared about the guy. So Ray's been seeing her all this time and never said—?'

'Oh, it's even more Charles Dickens than that, Jake. They haven't been dating at all. He's just been driving out to Mantorville once or twice a week to see if she needs anything. He's never asked for anything in return. Giving her time to finish her grieving, he said.'

'Jeez. That's so...' I couldn't think of a word that wouldn't sound embarrassing.

'Touching. I know. Especially coming from Stone-Face Man. Some time in the last couple of months he finally screwed up his courage to ask her out to dinner.'

'How do you know all this?'

'He's friends with a couple of my detectives. He worked a long time in Property Crimes, remember. They sit around with a six-pack on Friday nights and tell stories about matching up rifling marks and heel imprints.' He rolled his eyes up to express despair over squandered Friday nights.

'And they actually tell each other about their dates? Like back in Junior High?' Not for the first time, one of Kevin's stories was making me helplessly hilarious. 'Jeez, I can't remember the last time anybody told me good stuff like that!'

'You don't hang out in the right tree houses any more, Jake. You've been busy with grown-up stuff ... having a baby, getting shot. How's your leg, by the way?'

'It still forecasts the weather. Otherwise, better all the time.' He was with me the day we walked into that mess. He walked out, I didn't. 'So that's why Ray was so grouchy all weekend. They probably had something planned. Wouldn't you think he'd say something?'

'Not Ray. He's a soldier. What's he chasing, the Rutherford Strangler?'

'Worse. No, it's too messy to tell you about right now. Go on, figure out which two guys in your section have to go back out on the street and which newbies down the line have to get laid off entirely. Oh, and whatever you do, don't let anybody log any overtime. You hear me? Beginning today, overtime's out.'

'Jesus. I leave for three lousy days and you turn into the Wicked Witch of the West.'

'Not me. Blame Governor Pawlenty. He's the one that cut back on aid for cities and towns.'

'That isn't his fault. Obama didn't put enough zing in the stimulus.'

'Obama did the best he could,' Rosie Doyle insisted from the doorway. 'But the senate Republicans got fainting fits at the thought of giving money to anybody but bankers. Mitch McConnell, that's who's at fault.'

'Listen, if it wasn't for Mitch McConnell,' Ray Bailey said, walking in behind her, 'those tax-and-spend Democrats would have given away the store.'

'Tax-and-spend Democrats my ass!' Kevin

had one foot in the hall, but came back in to help raise the noise level. 'You think Cheney's stupid war in Iraq was free?'

We had been having this revolving-door conversation since February, and the end was nowhere in sight. The Bush administration had finally ended, and we had to pick somebody new to blame. It was tough, dirty work, but we were enfranchised Americans with grievances and we were going to keep at it till we got it right.

But not today, at least not in my office. 'Kevin, go away. Ray, sit down, we need to talk. Rosie, what do you need? The short version.'

'I hear you're revising the schedule.'

'Yes. What would you want if you could have it, which you probably can't?'

'See, this is the new Jake Hines administration style,' Kevin said, walking out at last. 'He's a hammer, and all the world's a nail.'

Rosie made a little shushing gesture at his back, staying focused as usual on her own concerns. She said, very fast, 'If we can't log any more overtime, will somebody have to take weekends?'

Was she eavesdropping on my brain? I'd been thinking that very thought. I hadn't said it out loud because I didn't see how we could tolerate being even more short-handed on two weekdays. 'Maybe. You saying that's what you want?'

'Yes.'

Why would she...? Something about Bo, probably. To keep from hearing about that, I said quickly, 'So noted. Anything else?'

'No.' She looked at Ray. 'BCA took the Mass card?'

'Yeah.'

Rosie shook her head mournfully.

'I know,' Ray said. 'I hated to let it out of my sight, but what can you do? I told them I'd raise hell if they lost it. I made it clear that it's the only thing we've got so far that's worth anything.'

'What are you talking about?' I asked them.

Rosie said, 'You know the victim's prints haven't turned up a match? He's not coming up in any arrest records nationwide. We're searching immigration now.'

'I heard.'

Ray said, 'And then we all thought the way they left the murder weapon there with him...'

'Looks like a pro hit,' I said. 'Does that surprise you in a drug house?'

'No,' Ray said. 'What does surprise me is that the gun is a Smith & Wesson .38 special – the Victory model.' He recrossed his legs, looking discontented.

'Oh, yeah? I don't know that gun. I've had the Model Fourteen for years, I used to use it for competition shoots . ..'

'Well sure, most of us did. But that was the Masterpiece.' He sighed, remembering. 'What a great weapon!'

'I had mine rigged out with a six-inch barrel and custom-fitted handgrips ... it was almost guaranteed to raise your score.'

'Right. But those old Victory models, you say you never fired one?'

'No.'

'They'd compare to the Model Fourteen like a Ford Falcon to a Cadillac. World War Two, they made about a million of them for the army, rough-finish cheapos. I see them sometimes in old movies. Some phoney like Dick Powell playing an asshole private eye sneaking down dark alleys alone at night.'

'You're saying it's not a very practical—'

'I'm saying it's been discontinued since about 1982 and no bad guy's going to walk into a dealer's shop this year and buy one for protection.'

'Somebody's collector's item, then. A stolen gun.'

'But not from here. Saturday afternoon, I remembered how Property Crimes guys been yelling about so many break-ins, and I decided to look brilliant and solve this case all by myself. So I searched their last two weeks' reports, thinking I'd come up with the .38 right away, but I got zilch. This morning I got LeeAnn to do a bigger search. She found no match in the last two years.' He rubbed his face. 'That gun wasn't stolen here. We're searching the five-state area now.'

'OK, pros from out of town. The victim wasn't wearing a holster, was he? It's not his own gun?'

'Don't think so. Far as I could see, his only weapon was an ordinary boot knife in a holster on his right leg.'

'A boot knife. Not likely we could trace that if it was stolen.'

'Which may have been the point.'

'Huh. So what's this Mass card you're both so hot about?'

Rosie said, 'Ray found the card buttoned into an inside pocket of that jacket when they took it off him. You heard how all the labels had been cut out of his clothes? He was trying to be a nonperson – but he was carrying this card. Soon as Ray showed it to me, I said it looks like the Mass card you get at a funeral. It's got a cross at the top, has a name and a date and a prayer – I think it's a prayer. But it's printed in some foreign language. Weird, strange lettering.'

Ray said, 'I showed it to Pokey – he got pretty interested, said he recognized the odd-shaped alphabet, he's pretty sure it's Ukrainian. He got a steno in the lab to come get it and make a copy for him.'

'But Pokey is Ukrainian. Wouldn't he know if it was his own language?'

'You'd think so.'

'Anyway, you've got to admit it's kind of interesting.' Rosie's eyes held a little sheen of excitement. 'Isn't it? A doper hoodlum who's stripped himself of all identity but carries one keepsake. Maybe something he couldn't bear to part with?'

'Or maybe it was left in the jacket by its previous owner, whose house he robbed?'

I saw her face set in stubborn lines that said she liked her own story better.

'Well, BCA will sort it out, I guess. Now, who's going to court with the prisoners?'

Ray said, 'Andy Pitman will take the tat freak – what's his name?'

'Hogarth Peter Weber.'

'Oh, right, how could I forget that? He's a real hard case, isn't he?'

'Yes. I'm hoping I've got the County Attorney pumped up to charge him with Murder One – no plea bargaining now, even if he begs.'

'The man annoyed you seriously, huh?'

94

Ray looked pleased. He likes to stick it to the malefactors. 'Rosie's going with the woman, and I want her to take Winnie along. I hate to spare both of them for two hours, but Winnie's got to learn these routine chores as they come up.'

'Agreed. My notes from the Gloria Funk interview are in the case file online, Rosie, and you can watch the DVD. She's willing to plead guilty to possession, even a little trafficking if the C.A. holds out for that. And she'll tell us everything she knows about the operation. In return, she wants some help with her habit and visitation rights with her daughter. Do everything you can to encourage that idea, will you? Try to keep her away from the boyfriend, because he'll try to scare her out of it. He's a snake.'

'I heard.'

'OK. Tell Andy, will you? He's got the bad boy of the outfit. He can find the very brief notes I made on Saturday after Hogarth Peter blew me off.'

'OK. You'll let me know about the skej?'

'When there's anything to tell you, I'll tell you.' Rosie has bulldog tenacity for anything she wants. The upside is, she doesn't pout. She fights like hell, wins or loses, and goes on. She says it comes from being raised in a house with many aggressive brothers. 'My

95

parents were too busy to baby me,' she told me once. 'In my house, you got what you could take and hold.' I can't speak for the truth of that family dynamic, but I know I've got one female detective sergeant who needs no looking after.

She went back to work in her own space, and Ray and I took an hour to sweat the new schedule. 'Let's take it a month at a time,' I said. 'What's the use projecting any further when nobody knows what's next?'

'God! Won't that be hard on everybody, though? Not knowing when you're going to be working.'

'Everything's hard on everybody right now,' I said. 'Nothing I can do about that.' A small inner voice congratulated me on sounding more like Frank McCafferty all the time.

In the end, we decided not to detail anybody to weekend duty. 'As it is, I'm working with a skeleton staff,' Ray said. 'What happens when somebody takes a training course?'

'You don't need to worry about that,' I said. 'Training's been put on hold throughout the department for all but new recruits.'

'Your good news is all bad news, isn't it? So from now on we'll make do with folklore, is that it?' He turned sideways and stood still in my doorway, peering at the door jamb while he said what was really bothering him – 'I guess you and I just stuck ourselves with weekend chores for the foreseeable future.'

'*Un*foreseeable,' I said. 'Everything is unforeseeable now.' I looked past him into the hall and added, 'Kevin's got to share the chores, too. And maybe Cathy Niemeyer could occasionally change *her* days off.'

'Well, but she waited years to get weekends—' He turned twenty degrees back toward me and inspected the bottom corner of my desk. 'How did you know...' He shifted the notes in his hands and said softly, 'God, this building ... everybody knows everything!'

'That's why we're all so tactful and kindly.'

He contented himself with a derisive snort.

I said, 'She's a nice lady and I hope it works out for you. I'm sorry I can't be more help with the schedule. Right now I'm just trying like hell to keep the doors open.'

'Yeah, right.' For a moment he sounded like the old Ray Bailey, grim and cynical. Then he took a breath and his emotions boiled over. 'You know I love my job. But once in my life I get lucky enough to have a chance with a wonderful woman ... I'm not going to let that get away.'

I'd supposed the story about Ray's gushy

97

Friday night conversations with the boys was one of Kevin's usual exaggerations. Now I realized it was straight reporting. Ray Bailey, historically the most circumspect man in Rutherford law enforcement, was panting to talk about his love life.

To avoid that clear and present danger, I grabbed up my desk phone and said, 'Oh, hell, what time is it? I promised to phone Pokey first thing this morning.'

Pokey only kept me waiting four minutes before he answered the phone call I had never promised him. As I was hoping, though, he had saved out one whole hour for what by his reckoning was a leisurely lunch. He graciously agreed to join me at an eatery near his office, after he'd maneuvered me into offering to buy. Comfortable years as a middle-class American doctor have never quite erased the cheapskate habits he formed in his hungry childhood. Pokey loves to freeload.

We wasted two whole minutes on greetings and menu questions before we got down to the body.

'Didn't need to do much testing to figure out what killed this fella,' Pokey said, tearing into the bread basket, buttering two rolls. 'Had six .38 slugs in him. They punctured liver and spleen, took chunk out of left

98

inferior lobe of lung and right atrium of heart, tore up the superior vena cava...'

'I hear you.' I grabbed a piece of zucchini bread before he spotted it. Watching Pokey eat always makes me feel the famine is at hand and I need to get my share fast. 'He was shot. What else?'

'And stabbed. Right here.' He drove an imaginary knife into his belly. I winced. His dissertation went right on, muffled slightly by a mouthful of crusty bread. 'Nicked top of pancreas, sliced edge of stomach...'

The waitress rolled her eyes sideways to watch him as she put down our Mexican plates. She walked away shaking her head, and I saw her mutter something to one of the other waitresses as their paths crossed.

I asked him, 'A knife like the one he had in that holster on his leg?' I meant, do you suppose they all carry the same kind of a knife? But Pokey vented a gleeful chuckle and said, 'Yah. Ray tell you about that? We ain't proved it yet – counting on BCA to find enough blood. Got crosshatch pattern on handle, looks like it mighta kept some blood down in them little ridges.'

'Wait, what are you saying? They stabbed him with his own knife?'

'Think so – Trudy gonna try to prove it. Looks to me like they wiped it off careful and put it back in holster. Pretty cool, huh? But I told Trudy – ain't no water in that garage, might be enough left for DNA sample.'

'So you think—' I wept into my guacamole as the salsa hit my palate – 'he was stabbed before he was shot?'

'Not much reason to stab a guy after you shot him six times, yah?'

'OK, stabbed first ... it kind of seems like he might have started the fight himself, doesn't it? Pulled the knife and gone after somebody—'

'Maybe. Them two druggies in jail tell any good stories?'

'The woman's stories are all about herself, and the man won't talk at all till he gets a lawyer.'

'And after lawyer even less. Well...' he spread sour cream over a mound of beef and cheese, 'you want to hear about victim's other health-related issues?' Pokey gets endless amusement out of American language glosses.

'Besides being dead, how much more does he need?' But he looked so pleased with himself I relented. 'OK, tell me.'

'First thing I noticed was lesions on scalp. Looked like some I seen before on older patient. Was exterior manifestation of metastasizing thyroid carcinoma. So when I got inside John Doe, I did careful scan of thyroid and found what I suspected – this fella had couple pretty good-sized nodules. Ain't got the tests back yet but ... I think whoever capped this hoodlum shoulda waited a while. Looks like he was already headed toward big lap dance in sky.'

'Your concept of Paradise keeps growing, huh?' He gave me a little pointy-faced nod and a wink. 'Would he have known yet, do you think?'

'Probably doing drugs, drinking plenty too from looks of liver, might not have noticed pain yet. But now, how about if wise old Ukrainian scientist gives you no-cost extra crime theory to chew on? Huh? Free clues – you like them?'

'Free clues are the very best kind, Pokey. And I'd be humbly grateful, as always. You want some ice cream to go with your gratitude?' I waved at our waitress.

'Sure. On top of pie is how I like it. You got piece of fresh peach pie back there?' he asked the dubious young woman standing at a careful distance from his elbow. 'Good, with two scoops vanilla, perfect. Peaches coming up from Georgia right now, Jake, so good they make you cry. Better have some.'

I settled for coffee. Pokey seems to have

some kind of permanent legacy from his barely survived childhood; he can pig out all he likes and stay taut as a drum. I was still trying to lose the eight pounds I gained waiting for my leg to heal.

'Ray tell you about his clothes? All labels missing? Wants to be Mr Nobody, recently arrived from Noplace. So clever – like nobody's gonna guess why alien thug does that. But Ray sniffed through jacket like bloodhound, found pocket inside lining with old dog-eared card looks like it traveled to moon and back. Sewn into seam so nothing shows from front, you dig? Very, very secret. Is good cop, ain't he? Ray.'

'The best.'

'Mmmm' He wolfed down another thousand calories and licked his lips thoughtfully. 'Is printed in Cyrillic.'

'Sir What?'

'Cyrillic. Named after St Cyril, old priest in Byzantium...' He waved old priests away with a bony hand. 'Tenth century sometime ... Cyrillic alphabet is basis for languages all through region where I was born. Ukraine, Serbia, Russia, Uzbekistan ... Lotta 'stans on old Silk Road. Nobody gave squat for 'stans till 9/11, now dictators from 'stans get White House dinners. Few crazy bastards over there wanna blow up America, so ... is good reason, yah? Get out best china, wines with French names, make trade deals, so maybe they put plastic explosives back in caves.'

'Thank you for that fascinating social commentary, Pokey,' I said, sneaking a peek at my watch. 'Does it connect back to the dead guy any time today?'

'What's this, upstart cop outa Dumpster gets little boost in rating and starts to think his time worth more than wise old Ukrainian guru?'

'Sometimes wise old Ukrainian gurus get a little long-winded and full of themselves.'

'OK, hard-nose, here's where it connects. Kids growing up around Chernobyl after explosion— You remember that, or wasn't you even born yet?'

'I'm thirty-five years old, Pokey, of course I remember Chernobyl.'

'Good. Then maybe you remember how many people living in path of fallout, especially little kids, were poor before and are now so poor they gotta beg for charity from Russians? You got any idea how poor that is? But you know one thing those kids got more of than other kids in whole world?' He leaned toward me and rasped, 'Thyroid cancer, baby. They got many times average world rate of thyroid cancer, and unusually high

103

number manifesting as follicular carcinoma – lesions on the scalp.'

'I'll be damned. Pokey, how do you know all this stuff?'

'Is regulation dermatologist stuff in school. After that, in US, we mostly forget it. But not me, because I read things on Internet from my part of world.'

'Which reminds me, what I wanted to ask you. The Mass card ... you told Ray you're pretty sure it was Ukrainian?'

'That's right.'

'Then how come you can't read it?'

He looked embarrassed. 'Well ... you want life story? OK, short version. Where I grew up, school was mile or so away ... I coulda walked. But we were so poor I never had shoes, some days no food. Was always gonna go next year. When I was eight, they resettled our whole village ... men went to work in Siberian forest.' He spooned up the very last of his peaches and ice cream, and sat back with a sigh. 'Couple of years later I ran away from there, went west with two older boys. My mother said go if you got somebody to go with, one of us should survive. Time I got to US I could speak Russian and German and French but couldn't read any language, knew how to sign my name was all. Adult education, in New York, learned English and

104

did twelve grades in three years. Got jobs and went to college, worked in hospitals, took med school at night. Never time to learn to read Ukrainian.'

I felt like buying him another lunch. To cover that sentiment I said, 'Maybe when you retire.'

'So I can go there on scenic tours?' He got a good laugh out of that idea. 'Listen, I ain't proved any of my ideas about where this John Doe came from, Jake, so don't hang your hat on it. Trudy's trying to find me lab full of smart postdocs might be interested in DNA from far-off lands. But you want my informed opinion?' He made an effete, snooty gesture. 'Is pretty likely your victim got himself into USA without signing guest book. And if Mr Nobody and hoodlums that killed him came from any of those East European gangs I saw in New York? Better be careful, my friend. You could be chasing some of meanest sumbitches in whole known world.'

FIVE

With three People Crimes detectives in court and most of the Property Crimes crew on the street chasing recently pilfered family treasures, the investigative wing got pretty quiet Monday afternoon. Ray and Kevin were hunched over their desks making flow charts and variable work schedules, figuring ways to stay afloat. I powered through a pile of paperwork and then, typing fast, summarized the two major cases we were working on – the homicide on Marvin Street and the rash of home invasions – in LeeAnn's newly created newsletter. She'd titled it neatly, *FYI: Investigations*, and given it a shortcut and a spyglass icon. I could hear Kevin's mocking laughter already, but trite or not it was easy to find and remember.

'This is such a great job,' I told her. 'I hope to bully most of our detectives into reading it before the first snowfall.' I'd walked out in the hall to deliver her attagirl right away, before I found an excuse not to. Not that I begrudged her the praise, but her gratitude for small favors was cringe-inducing, particularly since she was still stuck in her precarious perch in the hall where I'd 'temporarily' wedged her desk and chair several years ago. Everybody walked past her all day, bitching, asking questions, wheedling favors. It was amazing that she got anything done with all the interruptions she had to endure. As a result, though, she had become an informal clearing house for news and rumors and had a constantly growing array of corkboards and cubbyholes behind and around her desk, holding keys, notes, maps, and inside jokes. LeeAnn, I realized looking at her organized nuthouse, probably knew more about the inner workings of this section than I did.

'Do me one more favor, will you?' I asked, 'Try to find time to read this once a day, and let me know if we're all contradicting each other or if you see we've skipped something important.'

She was humbly grateful for the increased responsibility – she chose to see it as opportunity knocking. I got away from her desk right away, humble gratitude being one thing I can't tolerate even when I hold my nose. I have often wished I could transfer half of Kevin Evjan's self-esteem to LeeAnn, but until I figure out how to do that I don't spend much time hanging around her desk.

I gave her Pokey's autopsy report to scan into the log, and went back to my desk to type in his guesswork about the ethnic derivation of the victim. Then I tackled phone messages – the big sucking drain around which my day always seems to be circling. To get myself started I usually cheat, by answering the most interesting message first instead of sticking to chronological order. That day I pulled Bo Dooley's message out of the middle of the stack.

He was that rarity in the Rutherford Police Department, a transfer from out of town. We have more home-grown applicants than we can use, so we hardly ever take anybody from another system. But Bo came up from St Louis a year or two after the first big wave of crack cocaine hit town. He qualified with no trouble and was quickly hired by my predecessor because his specialty was drug interdiction. Rutherford was a mid-size town then, seventy-odd thousand mostly peaceable Midwesterners, hit with a sudden wave of explosive growth and the spillover from what we came to call the 'yellow brick road' – drugs following the river up from southern gateway cities.

About the same time, Minneapolis–Saint

Paul was changing from two busy cities into one burgeoning megalopolis, devouring its surrounding cornfields with new suburbs. The hundred miles of Highway Fifty-Two that used to separate Rutherford from all that action shrank to eighty, and with four lanes and higher speeds lost most of its buffering effect. Any Twin Cities criminal looking to expand his business could climb into an SUV and be on our doorstep in a little over an hour. Rutherford still looked the part of the bucolic farm center it had always been, surrounded by green acres of dairy cows and silos. But we were suddenly a long way from the shores of Gitche Gumee – we had to pull up our socks in a hurry.

I got promoted to head of Rutherford's rapidly expanding investigative division the following year, and Bo Dooley was an important component in the reorganization that followed. We split into two divisions, People Crimes and Property Crimes. I got a headman for each division, and Bo carved out a vice division in the middle, doing most of the legwork himself and getting help when he needed it from the rest of us. He jumped nimbly on board one of the other teams, too, if the cases piled up.

Bo more than carried his load, nobody complained about his work. But he was a hard blend with the rest of the crew – he didn't fish or hunt, or show much interest in team sports. He had a face that looked as if it would be right at home in a knife fight, and yet he wore small diamond earrings and offbeat clothes – he was different. Behind his back, some of the guys called him The Drug Czar. He was wrapped a little too tight – I kept waiting for him to go out a window without waiting to open it.

He came out one Saturday to help me when I found some crack in my golf bag. That's a whole other story – the point is, he came on his battered old Harley and brought along this tiny girl child in a pink helmet. He introduced her gravely as 'my daughter Nelly.' She looked just like him and behaved like three years old going on forty. That day I began to realize Bo was carrying an extra load he didn't talk about. Soon enough I learned what it was. His wife was battling a crack addiction, and the fight wasn't going her way.

Bo didn't give up easy. To be fair, I'm sure Diane tried hard too, but she was well and truly hooked. She would come back from a cure, more wraithlike every time, and try to reclaim her place with an increasingly stand-offish Nelly. Eventually some of her pals would visit in the daytime while Bo was at

110

work, and in a few days she's be gone again. Bo, with his face like granite, would be quietly putting the word out. Shortly after Nelly's fifth birthday Diane disappeared for the last time, and Bo filed for divorce.

'We can't do this any more,' he said. 'It's too hard on Nelly.' He was quieter than ever during the months that followed. Then he caused the first tremors in a personnel earthquake that was still shaking my section.

Months before the present budget shortfall, Ray commented that Bo seemed oddly critical of a sting we were planning. In particular, Bo thought that Rosie Doyle, acting as decoy, had insufficient security.

The first female detective in the Rutherford Police Department, Rosie did not so much break down barriers as fail to notice their existence. She had worked with Bo many times and had always held up her end. So why, Ray and I wondered, was Bo getting so antsy about Rosie's part in this particular operation?

When Rosie got hurt in the sting Bo had opposed, the air between Ray and Bo, which had never been cordial, turned rancid. That string of muggings culminated in a homicide, and we concentrated on that for a while.

Then I visited Rosie's hospital room and

111

found her locked in Bo Dooley's passionate embrace.

Grand as it is when people find happiness, two capable detectives finding it in adjoining cubicles in my department was about as welcome as a fast-spreading case of the mange. I knew at once that resentment and jealousy would swirl around the lovers. Morale would be affected, assignments would have to be reshuffled. On the street, did anybody think they would not be watching out for each other first?

Before I'd thought of half the possibilities, I got shot. By the time I got back at my desk and was ready to worry some more, Bo took the matter out of my hands. Standing just inside my doorway, he stared at his shoes for some time as if he suspected the laces might be going to explode. Finally he managed to blurt, 'I need to tell you I've put in my application to transfer to Domestic Violence.'

Unable to believe my ears, I said, stupidly, 'Oh?'

'Yes.' He inspected the thin sliver of sky outside my one small window. His mouth moved a couple of times but no words came out.

I said, 'You know, nobody around here is criticizing ... what's happening between you and Rosie.' Actually a small parade of detectives had come into my office, closed the door, and asked how did I plan to make this, you know, work? But for some reason I thought I owed him that lie. He recognized its base dishonesty at once and stared at his toes again in embarrassment. I made it worse, saying, 'I'm sorry if I've seemed disapproving. It's just – I don't know yet how it's going to work, I guess.'

'I don't think it will,' he said. 'So it's better if I work someplace else.'

'I don't exactly disagree. But – Domestic Violence? Isn't that a little like Derek Jeter signing on with the Rutherford Honkers?' The local semi-pro team was having a disastrous season, which only a faithful fan would notice was any worse than its usual season.

'DV crews get very few call-outs on nights and weekends. First responders mostly handle the initial incident and pass along the ones they think need follow-up.'

'I know. So?'

'So Nelly starts first grade this fall and I'd like to be home evenings and weekends, to see she gets started right.'

'Ah.' I looked at him, thinking, what's that got to do with what's going on with Rosie?

'It's hard for Nelly to ... she can't remember when she could count on her mom. So she's pretty ... um ... possessive ... of me. I'm

113

hoping if she gets a good start in school, makes some friends … it might get easier for her to accept Rosie.'

I looked at him standing there, ready to suffer some more, and wondered, why is it some guys can never catch a break? He finally had a healthy, capable woman to love, and now his daughter didn't want her in the house. I said, 'Well. How's it looking? For the assignment?'

'It just came through. I start in two weeks.'

'Damn. I mean, I'm happy for you but I can't replace you with anyone close to your level of experience.'

'Rosie's been helping me for a couple of years,' he said. 'She's good now and what she doesn't know I'll teach her.'

'That'll work, I guess. It better, because all retraining programs are cancelled for at least the rest of the year.'

'I know. They said at DV I'd have to learn the ropes from the crew that's there. The city's flat busted, huh?'

'Not to mention the state and the nation. Basic boot camp for new recruits, that's it. The rest has got to be monkey see, monkey do.'

'So,' Bo said, 'us old guys gonna finally get some respect, huh?' He gave me a tight little smile that hardly moved the rest of his face.

I have never subscribed to the notion I hear occasionally from crusty codgers that maybe another Great Depression might be good for us, take us back to the simpler life and the sharing they claim to remember from the Dirty Thirties. I can't speak for those far-off days, but I took a few knocks myself, growing up in foster homes in the seventies, and my impression was hard times make people harder. But driving home that afternoon past ramrod-straight rows of corn, I thought maybe the present fiscal calamity wasn't all bad, if I was right in believing that Bo Dooley had just made a joke.

'Dooley.' Bo answered the phone, in his new office, in his usual dry-as-dust voice. His telephone manner suggests he knows your call is bad news and is not surprised.

'Bo,' I said, 'you called?'

'About the woman I picked up at the grow house,' he said. 'Gloria Funk.'

'Oh, yes. I interviewed her in the infirmary later that day.'

'You did? Why? I mean, why you?'

'Things are a little mixed up around here right now,' I said. 'We're kind of taking the tasks as they come. What can I do for you?'

'Gloria was back in jail this morning and made her court date.'

'Rosie took her over, yes. I haven't heard yet what the disposition is. Where's her child, do you know?'

'CPS took her to Child and Family Services for the weekend. There's a grandmother – Gloria gave me her number but she was at work. She said she'd have to change her hours to take the little girl, so it will take a while. She wasn't at all eager to have her, but she said she'd take the child if we promised not to send Gloria. I assured her Gloria's going to prison, so – but then I got into court and found Rosie and the CA there pitching this story to the judge about the contrite mother who wants to reform and get her child back.'

'Gloria's willing to testify for the prosecution. I called Milo about her, I think they've already talked.'

'Well, Jake, did you see the house? You know she's been using meth?'

'Yes, but she's begging for help getting into detox. She's ready to tell everything she knows about the grow house. Milo's going to bat for her because she's his star witness. The broken nose is quite convincing.'

'Jake, she's an addict.'

'Right. Why else would she be living with an abusive drug dealer?'

'Well, do you know the odds against anybody kicking a meth habit? Why would you want to help somebody like that get her kid back?'

'Whoa, we're a long way from that decision yet. Besides, aren't you on the wrong side of this conversation? You're in Domestic Violence now, Gloria Funk's your client.'

'Sure. My job was to get her out of that house and away from the guy who was breaking her face. And I did that. But now she's trying to cast herself as a victim and avoid prosecution for dealing and possible murder. It's not my job to help her with that.'

'Bo,' I said, 'before you say any more I think you better have a chat with your supervisor because I believe you're trying to redesign the vehicle you're riding in.'

'Fat chance of that,' he said softly.

'Of what? Talking to your supervisor?'

'Yes. Well,' he said hastily, 'talk to you later.' And was gone.

I stared at my desk blotter for a couple of minutes after he hung up, feeling as if I'd just listened to the beginning of a train wreck and wondering if I ought to signal somebody down the track. Who, though?

While I was still pondering, Kevin Evjan strode back in. He was leading one of his newer detectives, the hockey player who looked about twelve. What was his name? 'See, he's just sitting there doing nothing,' Kevin told this fresh-faced kid. 'He might as well talk to us.'

'I'm ruminating,' I said. 'It's an important management skill.'

'I bet. You remember Gary Krogstad?' The kid and I mumbled pleasantries and they sat down. 'He's been on a high lope for the last three days, interviewing people whose houses have been broken into. Tell him,' he commanded; and Gary spoke up as if Kevin had pulled his string.

'The striking feature of many of these burglaries is how quickly they're being executed, often in daylight. People keep saying things like, 'I just ran down to the shopping center for my regular hair appointment, I was only gone for two hours.'

'I'm sure we've got a set of thieves who have somebody on the inside, Jake,' Kevin said. Typically, he'd insisted Gary do the talking but now he couldn't shut up and let him do it. 'They know just where to look. They get in, get the good stuff right away, and they're gone. No browsing.'

'We talking free-standing houses here?'

'Oh, you bet – the biggest, most expensive houses in town, the older elegant ones up on the hill, and the new ones out northeast. No condos for these birds, nothing but the best. They get in without doing much damage, give them that. It's like they know where the soft spots are, a basement window left open or a French door that's easy to jimmy. They steal very nice things, but at least they don't leave much home repair behind.'

'How about prints?' I asked Gary. 'They leaving any of those behind?'

'Techies haven't found a smudge. They must wear gloves every minute.'

'And have an accomplice working in a home service industry?' I said.

'That's what we think,' Kevin said. 'House cleaners, yard work, one of those. I've got two detectives out right now, getting lists of all services used by the last dozen home-owners.'

'Good.'

'It all takes time, though, damn it. How am I supposed to break up organized groups like this with fewer and fewer people?'

'You can't. You won't. Don't think ahead, just do this job today. What's next?'

'I got a lucky break,' Gary said, looking as if he just got a gold star in fifth grade math.

'Tell me.'

'One of the burglaries I investigated Satur-day, this woman had a set of three antique dolls, something called German Bisque –

119

that's something about the finish on the head. These dolls have beautiful clothes and wigs, they're worth thousands of dollars. The thieves got two of them, but the third one was in a different cupboard and they missed it. So she had a perfect example, and she let me take pictures and copy the document that came with the doll. We've all been studying it.'

'You should hear my guys,' Kevin chortled, 'holding forth about "white cotton bloomers, embroidered ecru collar ... "'

'We memorized the whole damn thing,' Gary said, 'right down to the buttons on the little leather shoes. And this afternoon, in the Reddi-Kash pawnshop out south of the Beltline, Wally's pretty sure he spotted the other two dolls.'

'Wally's my other Krogstad,' Kevin said.

'That's right, we do have two, don't we? You're brothers?'

'Twins,' Gary said. He looks even younger when he smiles.

'Awesome. Well, hey, guys, well done!'

'We been eyeballing that shop for a while,' Gary said, 'because one of the guys on patrol down there noticed that lately it seems to be unusually busy. So we got the sergeant to put it into BOLOs and leave it there a while.' Be On The Lookout lists get read out by the

120

duty sergeant at the start of every shift. 'Tell everybody, whenever you're down on the south side for any reason, drive by and watch it for a couple of minutes. We've seen some very nice merchandise passing through there. Gold jewelry, a lot of coins, high-end cameras.'

'It's an old shop in a run-down building,' Kevin said, 'always been a pretty sleepy place.'

'I remember the Reddi-Kash,' I said. 'Down on Southeast Twenty-First Street? It was there when I first started – I worked the graveyard in that section for one whole year. It was on the edge of town then, nothing beyond it but cornfields.'

'Rutherford grew around it since,' Gary said.

'For sure. Used to be run by an old guy named Ike. Wore sandals and walked like his feet hurt.'

'Still is,' Gary said, 'last I knew.'

'Slow nights in the winter,' I said, 'I used to stop in and shoot the shit with him. He'd give me whatever new skinny he had on the neighborhood, which in those days was kind of iffy. Seems to me there were a few beat-up rental houses, a bar, and a very messy machine shop ... a roadhouse a little farther out.'

'That area's cleaned up considerably now,'

Gary said. 'Got a C-Store, Chinese take-out place, beauty shop.'

'OK, enough memory lane,' Kevin said. 'What we need now is somebody to front some merch for us.'

'Oh, please,' I said, 'not another sting. Haven't we been stung enough for one year?'

'This isn't like the one you did before,' Gary said. 'Kevin told me about that. We don't need a team effort, just somebody to sell a few coins for us. And hang around the store for a while, watch what comes in.'

'Why can't you do that yourself?'

'I worked patrol on that beat till three months ago. Most of the people in the neighborhood know me.'

'I don't know. We already all have more than we can handle. I don't like the idea of taking on some offbeat—'

'We were thinking about Winnie,' Kevin said. 'She'd be perfect.'

'Winnie's just getting started in People Crimes. It's not a good time for her to—' Kevin had begun to wear a small self-satisfied smile. He sat and watched me, waiting for me to get it, and in spite of myself I began to see exactly what he had in mind.

Her name is Amy Nguyen. but everybody on the RPD calls her Winnie because when she started 'Win' was about as close as the chief could come to pronouncing her Vietnamese name, Nguyen. She is small and pretty and looks fragile as a porcelain cup. Actually she's descended from boat people and is almost as tough as the redoubtable grandmother who got her to Minnesota. No question, she'd be the perfect person to walk into the pawnshop with ostensible family treasures in her bag.

I said, 'We really don't have time for this kind of fooling around any more.'

'I'm only asking for one day.'

'Yeah, well ... ask Ray.'

'I did. He said if you OK'd it, he'd let her go for one day.'

'All right,' I said. 'If she's willing, one day.'

'But you don't have to do it,' I told her, an hour later. 'If you don't feel comfortable about it, say so.' Kevin and Gary had told her the story of the superfast break-ins and the dolls in the pawnshop. Pumped up and pleased with themselves, they brought her into my office to seal the deal.

She wasn't red-hot for it the way Rosie would be, but she didn't seem apprehensive either. After you get used to how small she is, the next thing you notice about Winnie is her poise – in the interplay of egos that is the Rutherford Police Department, she often

123

seems like the only greyhound in a yard full of Pit Bulls. She listened as they described the missing goods, and asked thoughtfully, 'You want me to stay under the radar or make sure I get noticed?'

Gary said, 'Get noticed how?'

'Go funky? Hair down my back and striped tights with hi-tops?'

Kevin's eyes lit up with joy – at last, a detective who shared his eye for street theater! When she helped us with the mugger last winter, he'd known Winnie as the marathon runner and martial-arts instructor who taught Rosie how to dodge. And she had been the decoy on the other team, the one we'd all hoped the mugger would pick, so that Winnie would get a chance to kick him behind the ear. That didn't work out, but the two women on the caper formed an unlikely friendship, and before long Rosie had persuaded Winnie to test for the detective division. She scored so high they made her take a couple of the tests over, and was ready and waiting to replace Darrell Betts when he went into the K-9 corps.

Now here she stood, showing Kevin that besides being strong and fast and decibels quieter than Rosie, she had a flair for undercover. I watched as he began to wonder how to get her switched to Property Crimes.

They took her into Kevin's office for a few minutes to get her ready for the assignment. Gary gave her a crash course in bisque dolls and described the long, dusty shelves and creaky wood floors of the Reddi-Kash pawnshop. Kevin got very involved in planning her outfit. He longed to see her in a brocade sheath and tight chignon, a sort of cut-rate Madame Chiang with a cigarette holder and strappy sandals. Winnie led him back to her original concept by telling him she had red satin hot pants to go with the hi-tops.

I answered a slew of emails and went back to the phone messages, trying not to get involved in any long-winded conversations. Now that I was Ben's ride home, I was antsy about my need to get out of there promptly at five. It made the last hour of work tense and tiring. I was beginning to understand the tightrope that is parenthood in our time.

At two minutes to five, holding the keys to my pickup, I was reaching to turn out the lights when Rosie Doyle appeared in my doorway and said, 'I'm going to kill Bo Dooley.'

'You'll have to do that on your own time, Rosie,' I said. 'We're too busy for unscheduled executions during office hours and we're strictly forbidden to clock any overtime.' I flipped off the lights and stepped into the hall.

'I'm serious,' Rosie said.

'I see that.' I turned the key in my door and heard the deadbolt slide into the strike plate. 'You seriously want to off the man you always knew was right for you but whom you never laid a glove on till his divorce was final?' I was quoting her directly, hoping to embarrass her out of continuing her present rant. 'That Bo Dooley?'

'Yeah. That one.'

'What's he done?'

'Screwed me up royally in court, while I was trying to do what you asked me to do for that Funk woman.'

'You want to walk out with me, tell me about it?'

'No,' she said, 'I want to stand right here and tell you about it.' She watched me take two steps toward the stairs before she turned and trotted after me. 'Jake? What's the matter, you mad at me?'

'No. But I have to go get my kid and try to get him home before he gets hungry and starts doing his siren imitation.'

'Oh, that's right, Trudy went back to work today, didn't she?'

'Yes.' I paused at the top of the stairs. 'You have to leave too. You got the memo I sent everybody, didn't you? The one about no more overtime?'

'Yes. I'm already clocked out, Jake, I'm just following you around the building because I feel I should warn you that I'm going to roast my fiancé over a slow fire. You know what he did? I can't believe this! You know what he did?'

'No. I thought you were going to tell me, but you're having too much fun yelling down the stairs. And I have to go.'

I took two steps down. She caught up with me and followed close by my side the rest of the way down, telling me the straight story, very fast, 'He came into court today after Milo and I had the deal all set up. We'd told Judge Tollefson Gloria had no priors, she was the victim of domestic violence. Explained that she was willing to cooperate on a guilty plea and testify for the prosecution. We said, "She's desperate to quit using and get her child back, Your Honor." The judge was buying it because he just wants to get his docket clear, what the hell? And her boyfriend was inadvertently helping our case, sitting there looking like a tattooed alligator...'

'Six minutes after five,' I said, pushing open the tall glass doors, stepping out into smells of hot asphalt and barbeque. 'Cut to the chase.'

'OK, OK – we had all the groundwork laid and we were asking for a suspended sentence on the dope and pleading the meth down to possession – she could be out in a few months, clean and sober. Then Bo walked in and took the stand to testify that he'd rescued her from the house with bleeding facial injuries. He was good, all quiet and businesslike, till we started talking about the plea deal and the process for getting custody back, and then – oh, God, Jake, he just went apeshit. He said, "Don't you people understand that this woman is a meth addict? You have any idea how close to impossible it is to break that addiction?" Sneering ... he as good as called the judge a fool and told the rest of us we were completely irresponsible if we even thought about entrusting a helpless child to a tweaker.'

We were in the parking lot now, standing next to my red pickup. I put my key in the driver's-side door and said, 'What do you want from me, Rosie?'

'Talk to him. Make him understand he's not a narc any more and he can't go swimming upstream like that.'

'I already did that.'

'You did?' She stared at me, round-eyed. 'When? How did you know he...'

'He phoned this morning to tell me he

thought we were wrong to be helping Gloria plead down her sentence. I told him he better talk to his supervisor because I thought he must have misread his job description. Look, Rosie,' I slid into the seat, 'why wouldn't Bo be dubious about this woman? His wife broke every promise she ever made to him.'

'I know. But he can't keep fighting the system like this, it won't work.' Distractedly, she began pushing combs back into her springy hair. 'God, when I think how good he was at the job he had. Come right down to it, I haven't done him any favors either, have I?'

I wasn't going to get into that swamp. 'Just talk to him, Rosie.' I started the motor, so she may not have heard the last thing I said. 'Try to get over being mad first.'

She was still standing in the parking lot, looking dissatisfied, when I pulled out. I drove to Maxine's house a tad faster than the law allowed. OK, ten miles over the absolute outside limit. I thought I could probably beat a speeding ticket if I had to, but I knew I couldn't head off Ben's penetrating wail of hunger if I didn't get him home in time for his six o'clock bottle.

Listening to Ben cry was still my personal equivalent of hanging by my thumbs from rusty barbed wire. Trudy kept telling me to get over it. 'Or if you can't stand the noise, give him that pacifier I left at Maxine's house.'

'Come on,' I said. 'And let him look like a retarded dork with that thing hanging out of his face? I'm not going to do that to my own son.'

'Then get used to it. It's just what he has to do to get what he needs,' she said. 'What would you do if you lost the power of speech?'

'Kick open a door, probably,' I said. 'I understand what you're saying, but it still feels like I'm being punished.'

'Poor pitiful Papa.' Goose pimples rose on her arms, though, and she shivered, rubbing them. 'Come here and kiss me, will you?'

I kept my arms around her after. 'What, are the pills giving you chills?'

'No, it's ... that word, I guess.'

'What, "punished"?'

'Yes. I've always hated it, and now that I have Ben' – she touched the edge of the kitchen cradle where he was sleeping – 'it makes me think of your story about Big Bad Red.'

'Don't,' I said. 'It was stupid of me to tell you about her. Just wipe her right out of your mind.'

I only told her the story because we were having such a good time, one Friday night last summer, drinking wine after dinner. To watch a beautiful sunset, we carried an extra glass outside and sat under the big trees. I told some silly jokes for the pleasure of watching her giggle, and then something she said reminded me of the second foster mother I had after Maxine.

A large ugly woman with no warmth and no luck, she had a deadbeat husband, who was mostly absent, and two children of her own just entering their teens and beginning to give her grief. Probably my reputation as a bad boy had preceded me. I was still very angry about losing Maxine, and she had plenty of long-standing grudges from a lifetime of drudgery. For those reasons and who knows what others, I hadn't been in her house ten minutes before we had each begun to circle the wagons.

I can't remember her name because I never spoke it. In my mind, I called her Big Bad Red. She said she was going to teach me some manners. I showed her by my sneering silence that I didn't believe she had anything to teach anybody. I should have given a little more thought to how uneven the contest was. I was a pretty healthy kid but I was only ten, and she was a big woman. Before long, knocking me around had become one of her few pleasures. I wasn't going to beg, and she wasn't going to put up with my attitude.

Luckily, before our toxic cocktail grew irreversibly lethal, Red made the mistake of giving me a cut lip one morning. She tried to keep me home from school, but I got away from her and ran for the bus. My teacher noticed my swollen mouth and took me to the school nurse. The nurse unbuttoned my shirt, found my bruises, and called the police. I spent some time in a shelter, grim but fairly safe, before they found me another foster home. I heard Red lost her license, which must have been inconvenient for her too.

'Nothing like that is ever going to happen to Ben,' I told Trudy, holding her, kissing her neck. 'We'll keep him safe.'

'I know. But isn't it weird how fast parenthood turns you into a wuss? I've never felt vulnerable in my life before. Now I think about safety systems all day long.'

'Tell me about it,' I said. 'I've checked the air in my tires so many times the guy who runs my gas station asked me if I thought my gauge wasn't working right.'

I pulled up in front of Maxine's house at twenty after five. The house on the corner was boarded up and silent. In Maxine's

132

house, I said a hasty hello/goodbye to Maxine and Eddy while I hoisted the little man out of his crib. He was just waking up, doing his usual greeting kicks and gurgles. Without pausing to admire them, I grabbed the big plastic bag full of diapers and bottles and the many products for keeping his tiny butt smooth, and humped the whole load out to my truck. When he was strapped firmly into the best child safety seat money could buy, I set out for the town of Mirium, forty miles distant.

It used to seem just a few tunes away – exactly right for a little decompression spin between work and home. That Monday night, as my son looked around curiously for five minutes, whimpered and gnawed his knuckles for ten, and then screamed at the top of his lungs for the remaining eighteen, I began to believe that the distance between Rutherford and Mirium was approximately the same as the width of the Sahara Desert at its widest point, and for the last few minutes of the crossing I would not have been surprised to see dying camels stretched out along the roadside.

I carried my desperately bellowing son into the house and handed him to my wife, who beamed at me as if I'd brought her a nice present. She was aglow. In two minutes she had Ben changed and contentedly drinking a warm bottle of milk on her lap. She told me there were potatoes baking, suggested I start the grill for chops. 'Then,' she said, 'why don't you open a couple of beers and come sit with me?' Her first day at work had been a smashing success and she wanted to tell me about it.

One good thing about parenthood, I was beginning to realize, was that it made police work seem predictable and easy.

SIX

Tuesday morning Winnie came to work looking like every teenage boy's wet dream, except for her expression, which was resolutely matter-of-fact. And because she's Winnie and everybody knows about her black belt, nobody whistled. But no work got done in any cubicle as she passed it, with those black-and-white-striped tights fitting her marathon-rounded legs like a second skin, the red hi-tops too funky for words below, and the red satin hot pants clinging to her taut little rump above.

She signed receipts for the three best pieces of unclaimed gold jewelry the department possessed, and hit the street. An hour later she was back, to get the diamond-studded wristwatch Kevin's grandmother had left him. He'd said she could use it on a second run if she was absolutely convinced by then that the place really did hold things for ninety days.

She just about knocked his socks off when

she told him she'd wangled a glimpse of the shop's back room.

'How'd you do that?'

'I told that absolutely vile manager ... Have you seen him?'

'Nice old guy with sore feet?'

'No. The one who's there today has one squinty eye and tobacco juice dripping out of the corners of his mouth.'

'Let me guess,' Kevin said, watching her face. 'He called you "honey"?'

'And "sweetheart".' Her face had turned into the mask of the Awesome Asian. 'So I told him I wanted to pawn the best thing I owned, but I'd only feel secure enough to do it if he'd show me some of his better treasures.' Snapping back into her lively American persona, she tossed back her shining yard of hair and grinned. 'Omigod, you can't believe the stuff ... and I saw the dolls,' she told a delighted Gary Krogstad.

She tucked Kevin's diamond wristwatch in her bag, freshened her lip gloss, and trotted away to take a second look at the pawnshop. While she was gone, as sometimes happens in a detective division, everything changed.

Kevin got a call about a burglary in one of the best southeast neighborhoods, and sent two detectives to investigate. Before they reached the house, the patrolman at the

136

scene called back. 'We need somebody from People Crimes, too,' he said. 'I just found an injured victim at the foot of the stairs.' Ray sent Andy, who soon called back for more help.

Ray and Kevin fed me details as the calls came in. According to neighbors, thieves had entered the house while the owners were out biking. Busily bagging up the family's extensive collection of rare coins and jewelry, they were interrupted by a teenage son unexpectedly sent home a week early from camp. Sunburned and loaded with dirty laundry, he bumped into them in the second-floor hallway. They evidently clubbed him with something, maybe a pistol butt, and threw him downstairs. Luckily a neighbor was in his back yard, saw the thieves run out the back door, and called 911. The first responders found the boy on the floor, unconscious, and called an ambulance. Nobody knew yet if his injuries were life-threatening.

Ray sent Clint and Rosie, stopped in my office to fill me in before he followed them, and told me to send Winnie along as soon as she got back from the pawnshop. 'She's not ready to be much help,' he said, 'but she should be in on this, learning the ropes. I have to get her up to speed fast, we need all the help we can get.'

'I know,' I said, 'I'll tell Kevin to send her right over there.'

Winnie came back with Kevin's pawn ticket about eleven o'clock and headed straight into his office. They came busting back out into the hall in about two minutes, both talking.

I keep my door open, so nobody knocks. They just walk in, often interrupting each other. It's messy but it works: I get the news while it's still fresh.

'Winnie thinks she's on to something over there,' Kevin said.

'Tell me quick, and then she's got to go.'

'There's this ... odd ... group of guys,' Winnie said, 'hanging around that shop.'

I said, 'Odd? How?'

'They stand around by the hour, talking on cell phones.'

'Winnie, that describes half the people in the United States.'

'Wearing the ugliest clothes I ever saw.'

'Oh, well ... in that case, book 'em, Dano.'

'They're very loud and pushy. Some of the calls ... I'm pretty sure they're not speaking English.'

'Oh? What do they speak?'

'I can't tell. Nothing I've ever heard before. It's harsh and guttural with a lot of...' She made sharp 'ch' sounds, like a hostile loco-motive.

'Huh. Were they pawning cameras and dolls?'

'Not while I was watching. But they come and go in very high-end cars. I ran the plates. None of them came up.' Winnie did a thoughtful hip-wiggle that stopped every-body's breath. 'Pawning things out of expen-sive cars? What's that all about?' She pursed her glossy lips and frowned, a look comically at odds with her outfit. 'They're adults, but they exhibit what I would call gang be-havior.' She cocooned inside herself for ten seconds, came back out, and said politely, 'I believe it would be in your best interest to have a look at these men, Jake.'

'I'll try, Winnie,' I said. 'But we've got a new break-in to deal with right now. Kevin told you, right? And Ray wants you over there right away. So what else? Did you pawn the watch?'

Winnie grew a tiny Mona Lisa smile. Kevin said, looking pissed, 'The slimebag only offered her two hundred dollars. Luck-ily I told her before she left, if it's anything less than five hundred, bring it back.'

'Did you?' I asked her.

'Yes. But just in case we wanted to take another look, I told him I was going to try the other shops and might be back.'

'Good! Well ... Winnie, have you got any other clothes here?'

'Yes. I'll change and go right away.' She took the address, and a list of items Ray wanted her to bring. While she was in the rest room, Kevin said, 'She's sure these guys at the pawnshop are up to something. How about I take her to the home invasion scene, with a quickie detour first so she can show me the men she's talking about? I could take Gary along, let him see if ... What?'

'You get too many people there,' I said, 'they'll make you for sure.'

'I could take the old van, park down the block. Close enough to see but not ... and for just a minute.'

'But doesn't this new home invasion sound like the MO you've been tracking?'

'Well ... yes.'

'And they couldn't be in two places at once, could they? So aren't you better off concentrating on today's break-in?'

'We can do both. Take a quick look at the shop and go right on to the house. Where I already have two detectives, by the way. If we get many more detectives over there, we'll be investigating each other's nose hairs.'

'True. OK, go ahead. Keep me in the loop, now.'

'Of course.' Winnie came out of the rest room in denims, with her hair in a braid, and began assembling the equipment Ray wanted. When she had it bagged, Kevin said, 'Here, let me carry some of that!' and yelled over his shoulder, 'Gary? Come out here.' The three of them loaded up and clattered off toward the freight elevator, Kevin talking fast, selling his plan.

They'd only been gone ten minutes when Ray walked into my office and said, 'Got a minute?'

'Sure. Are you back so soon because the house got too crowded?'

'No. We just about got the whole crew over there when the mother phoned back from the hospital to tell the dad that the boy was OK. A bump on the head but no concussion, she says. Dad cried with relief for about thirty seconds and then went back to being furious at his kid for getting thrown out of the Explorers Anonymous camp. He said, "My wooden-headed son has survived his first mugging."

'Maybe because he was so relieved the kid wasn't dead, he launched into this infuriated rant – said the kid has always been a Mama's Boy, that she protects him when he goofs up. "So," he says, "I paid for this big adventure that was supposed to straighten him out.

141

Bought a pile of expensive outdoor clothing, went through his suitcase when he was done packing it to be sure he wasn't taking any dope along. Now, I still have to be the one who takes him to the woodshed and beats some sense into him. And trust me, I'll get plenty of grief from my wife for doing it, too." I thought for a while we were going to have to take him to the hospital, he was turning purple.'

'Wow! So this time the break-in turned into home invasion aggravated by assault.'

'But luckily not homicide. I told Clint to stay and finish the report. The rest of them will come back as soon as they've had lunch.'

'You want to have yours with me in the break room? I've got about a gallon of Swedish stew.' Now that Ben was sucking up the little bit of after-mortgage cash that was left in our house, Trudy and I were brown-bagging lunch.

'And maybe darning socks and saving string before long,' Trudy said when she handed me last night's leftovers in a plastic container. Swedish stew is basically goulash without the paprika. Today's was long on pasta and short on meat, but thanks to Trudy's cooking it tasted good. We nuked it in the microwave and dug in with plastic forks.

'We caught a break in Friday's murder this morning,' Ray said. 'LeeAnn tried a different search, widened it from just firearms to all burglaries, and our Smith & Wesson Victory model popped up on a list of stolen items in Phoenix. I guess they hadn't got around to transferring it to the gun list.' He stared across my shoulder, looking bleak as only a Bailey can look, and said, 'I *guess* it's a break.'

'Except it means whoever popped that guy in the grow garage has quite a reach.'

'That's what I was thinking.'

'Have you talked to Pokey any more about that Mass card you found in the jacket?'

'No. I've been waiting to hear what BCA has to say about it.'

I told him about yesterday's lunchtime conversation. 'If his hunches are right about the sores on your victim's head ... maybe it would pay to have a conversation with the Phoenix PD about that Smith & Wesson.'

'Yeah. Maybe I'll try that.'

'Anyway, good for LeeAnn, huh? To think about widening the search.'

'Yeah. She gets better at her job all the time.'

'I know. I just went over and gave her an attagirl. I wish I could give her a little bump in pay, too, but—' My phone rang. As soon as I picked up the receiver, Kevin said, 'Jake, you have absolutely got to see these guys. Can you come over here right now?'

'Kevin, are you still at the pawnshop? Is Winnie still there with you?'

'Well, yeah,' Kevin said. 'We just got here, Jake, we've only been watching a couple of minutes. Are you coming?'

'Uh ... yeah, I can come in about five minutes. But hang on one.' I put the phone against my chest and asked Ray, 'They're still diddling around that pawnshop. You don't want Winnie to go to the home invasion now, do you?'

'No. Jeez, she's wasting the whole day, isn't she? It's always like this when Kevin mixes in.' He frowned, and the room seemed to darken. 'Tell her to come back here and get her new assignment.'

I told Kevin, 'The new burglary's taken care of. You three wait there for me.' They described where they were parked, half a block from the pawnshop, and I told them I'd park around the corner and walk to the back of the van. 'Watch your rear-view and open the back door when I get there.' I put down the phone and told Ray, 'She's got no way back till I get there. I'll go there right now and send them back as soon as I see what they're so excited about – it won't be long.'

The old Dodge van was parked a couple of car-lengths from the corner, on the right-hand side of the street heading west. The Reddi-Kash sign was big and red, above a dingy storefront across the street, half a block ahead. I stepped into the gutter when I got even with the van's back doors, and the right one opened before I could knock. I ducked inside, made my way forward through the seats and squatted beside Gary, back of the console. Kevin and Winnie were sitting in the two front seats, Winnie hunkered down so only the top of her head showed from outside.

Three chunky guys with whiskery growths that didn't quite manage to be beards were leaning against the iron window grate and pacing the dirty sidewalk in front of the store. Two of them were talking loudly, non-stop, on cell phones. The third was turned toward the shop, talking to a grubby-looking man with one squinty eye who stood in the half-open doorway.

Gary and Winnie were in the middle of an argument. 'No, it isn't,' Gary said.

'Yes it is,' Winnie said. 'That's the one I hocked the jewelry to.'

'He must be part-time help,' Gary said. 'I know this pawnbroker, he's an old guy with

145

sore feet.'

I said, 'Winnie, are those the guys you wanted me to see?'

'Yes.'

'Any of them inside?'

'I'm not sure. But do you see how they're dressed?' Two of the three wore velour exercise suits in sickening colors – one puce and the other a dark mustard like vomit. The third man, the one talking to the shop-keeper, wore jeans and the kind of clingy striped Ban-Lon shirt I thought went off the market some time in the late seventies.

'OK, they're not the fashion-forward set, what else?'

'I'm pretty sure they didn't buy those clothes here,' she said.

'Perish the thought,' Kevin said. 'Rutherford is legendary for the good taste of its male population.'

'Whatever.' She dropped her eyelids and flared her nostrils, the way she does when small jokes make her impatient. I forget sometimes how devastatingly humorless she is. 'But I don't believe they would find those particular clothes in stores here. And see the jewelry, Jake?'

All three wore heavy gold pieces – neck chains with pendants, pinkie rings, and the kind of massive watches sometimes favored by divers, that tell the time on four continents.

'Uh-huh,' I said, 'I think I see their cars, too.'

'That's right. The Cadillac Escalade and the Ford Excursion'

They loomed at the curb, glowing like beacons in a row of dingy older cars parked there. 'Man, that Escalade is some kind of red, huh?'

'It's called Infra-red,' Winnie said, 'I looked it up.'

While we watched, another bulky man in a baggy velour track suit, this one the purple of fresh bruises, came out of the pawnshop. He exchanged brief, surprisingly quiet, remarks with the three men lounging there. Then he and the man in jeans got into the Ford, drove toward us and on to the end of the block, turned right, and headed north.

'OK, I've seen enough,' I said. 'We can take down this shop any time, right?'

'Yeah,' Kevin said, 'but let's hold off till we figure out the connection with these workout enthusiasts we see here.'

'I agree. So let's all get back to the station. My car's around the corner, Kevin. Drop me there.'

My message light was blinking when I got back to my desk. 'What else is new?', I thought, and stood beside it, leafing through the new pile of memos and reports in my In Basket. Nothing there that couldn't wait. I'll go get a cup of coffee before I settle down, I decided, and turned toward the door just as Ray walked in, looked at my blinking phone, and said, 'You thinking of answering your messages any time soon?'

'Oh ... is that you blinking? I haven't— What is it?' He looked kind of fired up.

'I called the Phoenix PD about the Smith & Wesson. I found a People Crimes guy out there named Amos Healy, you know him?'

'No.'

'You heard about the kidnappings and shit they been having?'

'Sure.' The Phoenix crime wave had been making the national news for months. 'Mexican drug cartels, I thought they said.'

'Well, a lot of it is. But lately they've been seeing this rash of burglaries that seem to be more *refined* ... that's the word Amos used. I said what the hell's a refined burglary and he described some details that sounded familiar ... Is Kevin back yet?'

'I think I just heard ... here they come.' The voices of Kevin, Gary and Winnie reached the top of the stairs. I poked my head into the hall and said, 'Gary, come tell Ray what you told me yesterday about the burglaries you've been seeing.'

'That they're so fast and neat, you mean?'

'Yeah, that.'

In almost exactly the same words he'd used the day before – he must have had his written report memorized – he told Ray how quickly this band of thieves was getting into houses and finding the loot they wanted then getting out.

'Like they got some little helpers?' Ray was wearing his beagle look.

'That's what we been thinking,' Gary said.

'So I sent Chris and Julie out yesterday to interview some victims,' Kevin said. 'Looking for home services they might have in common.'

'Good. Good!' Ray said.

We all stared at him – Ray Bailey, beaming with enthusiasm. Was the moon blue?

'Gee, Ray,' Kevin said, 'I'm glad you're pleased.'

'I think you're absolutely on the right track,' Ray said, oblivious to the irony. 'This guy I've been talking to in Phoenix says they have started doing the very same thing. He said those Mexican drug cartels been keeping them so busy with kidnappings and drive-bys, shit like that, that for some time they missed the fact that a whole separate string of burglaries was being pulled off by what they now believe is a different gang. Very quick entries, precisely targeted on big-ticket items. Sounds familiar?'

'Oh, crap,' Kevin said. 'You mean these pests have cousins in Phoenix?'

'And maybe not only in Phoenix. My friend Amos out there says he's heard rumbles about a nationwide ring of East European immigrants – he's calling them the Mad Russians, but they're getting tips that they're probably from half a dozen countries in the old Soviet Union – that are into every kind of crime that will raise ready cash. Says he's got his lines out to narcs in other cities, guys he knows in Seattle and San Francisco, trying for more information. Out there they think this may be a nationwide thing, a group of East Europeans trying to muscle in on the drug trade, take some of it away from the Mexicans. It sounds kind of crazy, but— What have Chris and Julie found so far?'

'I don't know,' Kevin said. 'I just got back myself. Let's see if they're...' He strode down the long middle aisle of his investigators' work stations, stopped between two empty ones midway, and came back. 'I'll give 'em a call,' he said. 'I'll let you know.'

'Fine,' Ray said. 'Winnie, I think since the boy in the latest home invasion can talk now, you and I should go and ask him some questions.' He eyed the many bags and bundles she carried. 'What is all that?'

'The equipment you asked me to bring you,' she said.

'Oh yeah, at the house we're not going to any more.' He sighed. 'Stack it by LeeAnn's desk, we'll sort it out later. Come on, let's go.' He charged down the stairway, all his cheerfulness gone. Winnie dumped her bags, enlarging LeeAnn's trashy island, and trotted after him, inscrutable again inside her Awesome Asian persona.

Kevin got double-teamed right there in the hall by a couple of his auto-theft guys, determined to talk to him about a fresh pair of car-jackings. I heard him in his office asking plaintively, 'Both victims have what? Jesus, what now? A vampire?' He closed his door then and shut off the noise, and for an hour my office was so quiet I could hear LeeAnn hit the space bar on her computer. I powered through phone messages and put some details about the latest break-in into our daily journal. By four o'clock, I was looking at an almost clean desk.

Then Milo Nilssen walked in and said, 'Aha!' It's one of his favorite things to say.

'What?' I said, wishing I didn't have to hear his answer.

'Clearly, the city can make its first cuts

right here. Look at that desk, there's hardly anything on it.'

Milo's alternative needling tactic, if he catches me in the middle of a work spasm, is to rant about the piles of paper all around me, that prove I can't organize my job properly. He has picked up a lot of self-confidence since the scandal that catapulted him into the County Attorney's job he was never going to get otherwise, but he's still got a little edge of uncertainty that makes him need to plant a gotcha on somebody before he can start a conversation.

'You're too late,' I told him. 'I already lost three detectives. You?'

'Only one attorney, so far. But then I only had three to begin with. Oh, and one of my stenos has to go to four days. I'll lose her if she can find a decent job someplace else.'

'The upside is, she won't be able to.'

'Isn't that a splendid path to workplace stability? We're keeping people in their jobs because otherwise they'd starve.'

'They're no worse off with us than with anybody else,' I said. 'The county can't put the next two years on its Visa card, Milo.' I was getting so schooled in this debate I could automatically switch to the opposite side of whoever started it.

'Yeah, yeah, yeah. I just came by,' he said,

getting a little gleam on, 'to tell you that the Funk woman is getting all the mercy you requested, and a spot over.'

'She is? I thought— I heard that Bo...'

'Tried to throw a great big monkey wrench in the plan. You heard right. What the hell's he doing in that job, anyway? Talk about a square peg in a round hole.'

'He's maybe having a little trouble adjusting...'

'You think?' Milo rolled his eyes up.

'But he'll get the hang of it. Bo's a very capable officer.'

'Right. But just as a policy matter from now on, Jake, any screw-ups you're inclined to treat kindly, I suggest you send them to court with Bo Dooley.'

'OK. What about Gloria?'

'She made out like a bandit. Her boyfriend got his bail set at half a million dollars, but the judge was so annoyed by Bo's performance in court that he dismissed Gloria's marijuana charge entirely on the spot. Anyone could see, he said, that Ms Funk was not reaping any handsome profits in the drug trade. He gave her three years suspended on the meth rap on condition she immediately be remanded to a treatment center in the custody of the supervisor. Visitation rights with her daughter to be adjudicated as soon

153

as the mother's recovery is deemed to be well in hand.'

'That's what he said – "deemed to be well in hand"?'

'His very words. You know Judge Tollefson. Why issue a pompous opinion when with just a little more work you could make it truly grandiose?'

'So she's going right into detox?

'Yup. Drying out at Fountain Center at the taxpayer's expense so she can get her groove back and try it all again with somebody new.'

'You seem a touch more cynical than usual this afternoon, Milo. Anything in particular eating on you?'

'Nah.' He shot his cuffs, smoothed his hair, and tightened the knot in his tie – a replay of his old bag of tics that I hadn't seen in a while. 'It's just ... when the pie starts getting sliced a little smaller, the motivations show up plainer, I guess.'

'You think I had something to gain by recommending leniency for Gloria Funk?'

'I didn't say that.'

'You seem to be implying it.'

'Jeez, don't be so touchy. No, in your case I just think maybe having a baby has softened your brain a little.'

'In my case? Am I on trial for something?'

'No, Jake.' He got up and buttoned the

ridiculously dignified double-breasted jacket of his suit, shrugged a couple of times to settle it smoothly over his broad shoulders, and picked up his briefcase. 'You are not on trial, and neither am I. See you.' He strode out with his cheeks a little pinker than usual.

I looked after him wondering what the hell that was all about.

Milo and I used to mix it up like this all the time. Lately we'd been getting along better, but something about the Gloria Funk hearing had put us both on the defensive. That was pretty stupid – neither one of us had a dog in her fight.

Except, come to think of it, maybe Milo didn't appreciate getting second-hand suggestions from the investigative division about the disposition of a prisoner. Especially when they got transmitted by a detective whose pay grade was several ranks lower than his, and who was not renowned even in her own department for exceptional tact and diplomacy. Why the hell hadn't I thought to phone Milo and share some information in advance, instead of getting him steamrollered by Rosie in court in front of a judge who I now remembered always did his best to make Milo look like a turkey?

And if Tollefson did that to the County Attorney, how much worse had he probably made Bo Dooley look on his first trip to court in the new job?

Shit!

It was only a quarter to five, but I decided I'd done enough damage for one day. I locked my office, drove to Maxine's house at a moderate speed, and still got there by three minutes to five. Maxine was on the couch, reading aloud to all her kids. She looked at the clock, surprised.

'Finish your story,' I said, 'I don't need any help.' I heard her voice going on about green eggs and ham – how many thousand times had she said those words? I wondered – as I walked into the bedroom and loaded up. Ben was still asleep. He stretched when I picked him up, but didn't open his eyes. I cradled him on one shoulder and slung his gear over the other.

Maxine read the last nonsense repeat by Dr Seuss as I walked by the couch. She closed the book and said, 'I delayed his afternoon bottle a little today, Jake. I'm hoping that'll keep him more contented for the trip home.'

'So far it's working,' I said. 'Thanks.' I strapped him into his carrier and drove sedately north on the highway in glorious silence. Ben didn't even open his eyes for the first twenty miles, and he was only just

156

getting down to serious knuckle-gnawing by the time I reached the Mirium turnoff. Trudy wasn't home yet, but I'd passed Formula Prep 101 and was cool with that chore. Ben and I were in the rocker, guzzling milk and beer, and listening to the news, by the time she walked in.

'You two look pretty contented.' She smiled and put on one of those big white aprons she wears to cook. 'I decided I'm hungry for hash browns. With a cheese omelet, how does that sound?'

'Wonderful. Did you talk to Maxine?'

'About a later bottle? I asked her to try it, yeah.'

'Well, it worked tonight. I don't know how much crying Maxine had to endure this afternoon, but I got all the way home without a squeak.'

'Good. He's wide awake now, though. Look.' Ben had drunk all the milk in his bottle and was lying still, looking around. Trudy held out a finger and he grabbed it, kicking and gurgling.

'How about that?' I said. 'All relaxed and enjoying the sights. Sort of ... touristy.'

She laughed. 'His eyes are starting to really work, I guess. Fun, huh?'

'Ozzie Sullivan said the other day, "Another couple of weeks, he'll start telling you what you're doing wrong with the car.'''

'Oz should really throw his oldest child down the well and leave him there for about a week.'

'I wonder if he's tried that. I wonder if we'll ever have to?'

'Aw,' she kissed Ben Franklin's tiny cheek, 'of course not.' She slid her finger out of his iron grip. 'I better get to work on those potatoes.'

'I think we'll go out and take a look at the garden.'

Friday's wind had blown some trash in, but when I cleaned it up over the weekend I was pleased to see that it hadn't damaged the corn crop. It was almost knee high, with ten days still to go to the Fourth of July (the Minnesota measure of gardening success). The potatoes were getting pretty buggy, though. I was going to have to spray.

'I think,' I told Ben, 'next year we should put the peas where they'll get a little more sun.' He waved his tiny fists and kicked like he thought talking about vegetables was a ton of fun. So I told him about my plans to shore up the tomatoes on a taller stake next time. He perched on my knee and watched as I pulled a few weeds out of the carrots, and gurgled approvingly when I told him they should really be thinned by the following weekend. Mourning doves were singing their soft dirges in the barn by then, and the sun was a red disk sliding behind Dan Cassidy's windbreak. Ben fell asleep on my shoulder as I carried him back into the house. The hash browns smelled like a hungry man's dream.

SEVEN

Wednesday morning, Rosie Doyle walked up behind me as I unlocked my door and said, 'Ray and Kevin are waiting to talk to you, but can I sneak in ahead of them if I'm quick?'

'Sure. Come on in.' I plunked my briefcase down by the already-blinking phone. 'Sit. What's on your mind?' She looked a little more electrically charged than usual; her bright red hair was doing that spiraling-toward-the-moon thing it does when she gets nervous and can't keep her hands out of it.

'I'm following up on the drugs and gear from the Marvin Street house. I thought the new equipment for the meth lab would yield the quickest results because it's all still in the packing cases. So I got the Board of Health guys to let me copy the labels as they loaded it on to the truck.'

'I heard. Good for you.'

'Yeah, well, that's what I thought. So I

160

started tracking backward on the shipping stickers and bills of lading, looking for some suppliers to talk to. I thought I could squeeze their toes a little and maybe round up the buyers.' She kept rearranging the pile of papers on a clipboard rested on her knee – or not rested exactly, held captive in a nervous grip was more like it.

'Sounds reasonable. How's it working out?'

'Up to a point, fine. I've determined that all the equipment and supplies arrived at the railroad depot in Rutherford within a period of about ten days, early this month. Shipped from an address in Queens.'

'Picked up here and signed for?'

'Yes. You want to see the signature?' I didn't, but she shoved it under my nose anyway – an illegible scrawl.

'Where's the— Don't they usually make you print your name, too?'

'They did. Here.' Far down in the corner, in primitive block letters, Kerajic or Kreutch or maybe Klimt. The first initial could be H, I thought.

'Not much, huh? Where's the name of the company? Is that it? Kind of smudged.'

'Under a bright light you can see that it says Bestway Agricultural Supply Company. Which is a company that doesn't seem to exist in Queens, New York. Especially not at this address here,' she tapped it with her pencil. 'Which I'm told by the New York Postal Authority would be somewhere in the middle of the East River.'

'Ah. Have you talked to the Board of Health? Here, I mean.'

'Yes. Their response is quite ... bureaucratic. If I hand this problem back to them, they will turn it over to their investigative wing. Or arm? The person I talked to didn't seem to know where that is but she'll find out. If I want her to.'

'Have you talked to Bo?'

'No. I thought' – she looked at her toes – 'that maybe I shouldn't bother him at his new job.'

I opened my mouth to say, why don't you just turn over in bed and ask him? But her closed face told me not to go there, so I said, 'Well, I think your hunch was very good that the meth lab is the best place to start. So if you don't want to ask Bo,' – we were carefully not meeting each other's eyes by now – 'go back to Ray and let him decide if he'd like to talk to Bo. Otherwise, ask him which federal agency he wants you to call for help. I think Bo usually took stuff he figured was too heavy for us to the DEA, but it's up to Ray now.'

'Yes,' she said. 'I was hoping to handle this for him, since he's so busy, but ... well. I'll ask him what he wants to do. Thanks.'

'Also, there's a lab ... Ask the BCA, they may have already sent some samples there. The lab I have in mind analyses marijuana, tells you what strain it is. Sometimes that gives you a lead on where it came from. I'm sorry I can't be more help, but Bo's been heading up the narcotics investigations for quite a while so I haven't had to get into the details.'

'I understand. Thanks for your time.' It was so unlike her to be formal and correct that I just nodded, at a loss for words. Rosie was deep in the weeds, no question. Watching her walk away with her back very straight, I wanted to tell her, 'Everybody fights. It goes with the territory. Apologize, it won't kill you.' But I was two days behind entering employee hours and benefits in the spreadsheet Frank was making us keep, the budget estimates for the next half-year were due by the end of the week, and I suspected that ancillary tasks like relationship counseling should probably be left to people who knew what they were doing. When she got to the doorway, I said, 'Tell Ray and Kevin to give me ten minutes and then come on in.'

I got all but one of my phone calls answered before they walked in together, already talking.

'The TV reporter on the news last night said something about "the latest in a series of home break-ins,"' Ray said. 'Mrs Anderson's not much of a newspaper reader, so she didn't know there were any other home break-ins until she heard that. Now she says it's an outrage that these people are being allowed to "run around loose". Like we had a perfectly good leash for them and we neglected to use it!' He flopped into a chair in front of my desk and glared at my blameless phone.

'Let me guess,' I said. 'Mrs Anderson is the Mama's Boy's Mama?'

'Of course,' Kevin said, 'and being an avid cliché collector she has bought into outrage. She discovered it during the uproar over bonuses for Wall Street bankers, and now she's going to be outraged often, until the fad passes. This week, when her dimwit son went off the reservation at that camp they fobbed him off to, he got sent home just in time to get tossed on his head. Now that's an outrage, and we're to blame.'

'People want somebody to be at fault, nothing new about that,' I said. 'Is he out of hospital yet?'

'This morning,' Ray said. 'The docs are

firm about it, he's fine. But of course Mama Anderson has her doubts.'

'Yeah, well— Where are you with everything else?'

'It still feels like I'm making this up,' Ray said, 'but all the evidence says the burglars Kevin's chasing here in Rutherford are in some way connected to the ones Amos Healy is looking for in Phoenix.' Kevin, sitting beside him, nodded in a rare show of unanimity.

'Because of the gun, you mean?'

'And because the burglaries are so nearly identical.'

'Always three or four guys with an uncanny knack for breaking into buildings,' Kevin said, 'and getting out fast.'

'Like in both places they're paying some local service person to tip them off when the houses are clear, huh? Did they get away with anything at the Anderson house, by the way?'

'No. They heard the sirens coming and dropped it all in the back yard before they jumped in their cars and took off,' Kevin said. 'It's the first break we've had – and the first time in this string of break-ins that anything's ever interrupted their routine.'

'Including in Phoenix,' Ray said, 'none of them have ever made a mistake, till now.

They know when people are out, and they know just where to look for what they want. Amos says it's like they've got a self-help book called *How to Pillage the Village.*'

'I like our theory better. You sending the stuff they dropped to the BCA.?'

'Oh, you bet. Plus the sack they were carrying it in. I don't really expect to get a fingerprint, though – they've been very careful about wearing gloves.'

'If they were fleeing the scene, though, it could happen. How are Chris and Julie coming along with that report on home services?'

'They had a couple of houses still to go,' Kevin said. 'I'll have it by noon.'

'Let me know. What about the Mama's Boy?' I asked Ray. 'Did you get him to talk?'

'Hey, try and stop him. Mama's Boy has a story now. His father sends him out to have his first big adventure, pays his way on some kind of a quest that's supposed to make a man of him. But he screws up as usual, gets caught using some controlled substance that he managed to procure out there on the dusty trails. Gets sent home, and there's his first big adventure waiting for him in his own upstairs hall. He's talking about Kismet!'

'Sure puts a positive spin on getting dumped on your head.'

'Doesn't it? He says it's turned him into a

true believer – the Lord's sent him a message. The boy's going to turn his life around.'

'Well, you said yesterday it needed turning.'

'According to his father.'

'Did you believe him? About seeing the light?'

'I don't know. His mama certainly does, she says he's...' Ray opened his little notebook, thumbed the pages, and read, '"At peace in a whole new way." It's a heartwarming story.'

'And a great way for him to change the subject from whatever he was smoking. How did he get it out there on the trail, by the way?'

Ray looked mortified. 'I should have asked him that – but she was right there, and everybody was so dazzled by his epiphany.'

'Uh-huh. Epiphanies'll do that. Does he remember anything at all that might be useful?'

Ray's expression grew thoughtful. 'He said they talked funny.'

'Is that a fact?'

'Yeah. The three big tough guys who threw him over that stair railing yelled something to each other he couldn't understand. Does that sound familiar?'

'I feel like I'm on some stupid Mobius

167

strip,' Kevin said. 'We run around and around it and keep hearing the same things over and over.'

'Ray,' I said, 'did Mama's Boy—What the hell's his name, anyway?'

'Ricky.' Ray's lip curled. 'Doesn't it figure?'

'Yeah. Did Ricky happen to say if they were wearing velour warm-ups in disgusting colors?'

'Now, see, there you go again, Jake! That's what Winnie asked him. Ricky said he noticed they were wearing funny clothes, but he couldn't remember any details. So I asked her, "Why are you asking him that? What's that about?" And then she told me about the men at the pawnshop.'

'Did she do her imitation of how they talk? The bad-suit guys? Did she do that for Ricky?'

'Yes. Ricky said he wasn't sure.'

'Ray – now *I* feel like I'm making it up – but you seem to think our bad-suit guys are connected some way to the Mad Russians in Phoenix?'

'I'm starting to buy into that idea. Yes.'

'But then – I know this keeps getting crazier – is it also possible they're the ones who shot the John Doe in the grow garage? Is that what you're thinking?'

He shrugged. 'I'm beginning to think anything's possible.'

'Well, but— The same four guys doing all this bad stuff at once? Burglaries and murder, corrupt deals with pawnbrokers, and two or three access points into the drug business? It sounds too ... busy.'

'We don't really know how many of them are here. Or what their connections are. Lately it seems as if Big Crime is morphing into something that looks like Big Turf Battle.'

'Kind of like Walgreens putting up stores on all the good corners?'

'I hadn't thought of it that way, but actually that seems to be what's happening on the Mexican border. Big gangs, cartels, putting markers down. My corner. Yeah.'

'Rutherford's not big enough to support that size operation. Why are they here?'

'Well – go back to the Walgreens example. They often build on corners and hang on even when the neighborhoods they expect to fit into aren't going to get built for four or five years.'

'Jeez, are drug dealers as rich as Walgreens now?'

'Well, they're not playing by corporate rules, remember – they can do very creative bridge financing. Amos Healy says some of the Mexicans out there in Phoenix are bankrolling their drug start-ups by doing kidnappings first. They grab people and torture them, put them on the phone with their relatives and let them scream and beg for help. Then the bad guys go collect the money and drop their half-dead victims by the roadside. Amos said we should be grateful if they're only doing burglaries here.'

'OK, I'm grateful. How are we going to prove any of this?'

'Catch them at it,' Kevin said, 'and squeeze their balls.'

'You know,' Ray said, frowning out my window, which was too high and small for him to see anything but sky, 'it's too damn bad you didn't have a wire on Winnie when you sent her into Reddi-Kash to hock the gold stuff.'

'Yeah, well, that's easy to say in hindsight,' Kevin said. 'We didn't know she was going to find these funny-talking guys and their cell phones. I just wanted her to find out if I should yank the license on that pawnshop when I was ready.'

'Which you certainly can, but now we don't want you to,' I said.

'What I'm thinking is if we had a recording of those guys, we could play it for Ricky,' Ray said. 'If he'd say for sure the bad-suit guys were the ones who threw him downstairs, we'd be pretty sure they were also the ones that hocked the dolls, right?'

'Better still,' I said, 'we could play it for Gloria Funk. If *she* recognized the voices we'd have our murderers.'

'Well,' Kevin said, 'you know I do still have my grandmother's watch.'

'You don't have to do this,' I told Winnie again, after lunch. 'If you're not comfortable with it, you should say so.' But with a detective on either side of her looking at her as if she held the keys to the entire justice system, it wasn't exactly a value-neutral question.

She didn't seem apprehensive. Although to tell the truth, a lot of the time it's hard as hell to tell what Winnie does feel. At that moment, I thought she just looked like somebody deciding what to have for lunch. She sat with her small feet not quite touching the floor, considering. After a few seconds she said, 'I think I should wear different clothes.'

'Oh? I thought what you had on before was very ... effective,' Kevin said.

'Something a little more businesslike,' she said, staring into the middle distance, essentially talking to herself. 'Like I'm getting ready to do something and there's no more time for fooling around. The navy blue suit with the mini-skirt, I think. Red platforms.

171

Pearls.'

'Whatever you think,' Kevin said, looking more and more dazzled.

I met Ray's eyes and saw that he shared my unease. Were the two of them having too much fun with this? 'Winnie,' I said, 'remember, that guy in the grow garage is still dead.'

'I know. I'll be careful. How do I work the ... um ... recording device?'

Ray sent her home to change clothes first and then took her to the Emergency Response Unit to get wired up. Their lone female member was not on duty that day, so Ray came back and got Rosie to help Winnie with the taping. After half an hour, they came out of the bathroom insisting that the wire was firmly secured somewhere under her skimpy little suit. Rosie, who seemed greatly cheered by working with Winnie, showed me proudly how she'd sewn a tiny camera into the flap of Winnie's shoulder bag.

Winnie tucked Grandma Evjan's precious diamond watch into the bag next to her Glock and her shield, and headed out again for the pawnshop. I didn't see her go, because by then Kevin had sent Chris Deaver and Julie Rider into my office to tell me what they'd learned about the people who serviced the burglarized houses.

'We talked to ten home owners whose houses have been robbed,' Chris said. 'What showed up was that all of them routinely use the services of one of two companies.' I leaned forward, listening. Everything about Chris Deaver is soft – his voice, his hands, his well-fed middle spilling over his belt. Part of his effectiveness on the street is that strangers take him for a nice, harmless dork. The shark elements in his nature never surface till they're needed.

'The first one's Home Cleaners. It's just what it says it is, a company that employs teams of workers to clean houses. Most of their personnel have been with them for years, they say, and their client list is also very stable. But they service six of the ten houses that have been ransacked in the last two months, so we have to think there could be something going on there.

'The big surprise is that the second one is Aarsvold Yard & Garden. Who'd a thunk it, huh? Must have planted half the trees and hedges in Rutherford, haven't they? But it turns up on the list of service firms at seven of the ten households.'

'Oh, but I can't believe Aarsvold's would be involved in any funny business,' I said. 'Do you buy that, Kevin?'

'Well, I'd love to pin *something* on the geniuses who built that abortion around Silver Lake,' Kevin said.

'The No-Fly Zone?' Chris chuckled. 'You can't blame Ole for that. He just built what he was told to build. He told me, 'The city fathers wanted the geese dispersed, and a job's a job.'

What had started as a rest-stop on the Canada goose flyway had evolved, over many years of unintended consequences, into an enormous year-round population of freeloading geese swarming all over a sweet little man-made lake, fighting and feeding and fornicating, killing the grass and paving the shore with excrement. The birds were a source of pride and pleasure to a lot of people and in time showed up in advertising brochures and the names of athletic teams, but finally the city had to face the fact that, while a few geese look pretty on a lake, a vast honking swarm of them is a pestilential mess. So Rutherford paid Aarsvold Yard & Garden to build two fences around Silver Lake, plant grass between them, string wire between the fences, and then hang strips of tinfoil from the wire to flutter and scare away the geese. Some of the geese did fly away, and others dispersed up and down the river, leaving us to ponder the fact that while too many geese on a lake are ugly, a forty-foot-wide strip of silvery, fluttering no-goose-land is not a thing of beauty, either.

I didn't want to let the birdshit jokes get started, so I said quickly, 'You must have other candidates besides Aarsvolds, don't you?'

'Not really. All the other firms people mentioned just turn up once or twice. But Home Cleaners service six of these houses, and Aarsvolds do regular work at seven.'

'Obviously there's some overlap,' Julie Rider said. Yin to Chris Deaver's Yang, she looks as buffed up, sharp and disciplined as he is disheveled and mumbling. They almost always work as a team, and it remains one of the wonders of the department how well that arrangement works. 'Three of the houses use both services. Including the latest break-in, the Andersons.'

'Hell you say! But that's the only one so far that's included an assault, right?'

'Right. And that was just an accident, I guess – the kid came home when he wasn't expected. In that way it doesn't fit the pattern at all, and we thought about throwing it out of the sample, but—' Julie looked pensive.

'Why would you throw it out?'

'Because at all the others their intelligence

seems to have been so good. In every other house on this list, they seemed to know exactly when they could go in safely.'

'And it almost has to be from occasional help like this, right?' I said. 'Nobody has full-time servants any more – not in Rutherford, anyway.'

'That's right,' Julie said. 'These thieves can't be getting calls like "OK he's gone, you can come in now." So that's the other thing we've started asking people – where did you go that day?'

'And it turns out,' Chris said, 'that's exactly the kind of information they're getting tipped off on – regular hair appointments, or a golf game that's always played on Tuesday. Just the kind of thing occasional helpers could become aware of.'

'At first we thought it was too far-fetched,' Julie said, 'that they couldn't have that much information. But it's so consistent – Kevin's told you, hasn't he, Jake, how quickly they get in and out?'

'Everybody's told me that – slicker than snot, Gary says.'

Julie winced. 'Yes, well, that's ... precise enough.' She loves the puzzle-solving aspect of her job, and the community service, but finds the gritty parts taxing.

'So, in the end, what made you decide to

keep the Anderson house in the sample?'

'Because the way they went about the burglary does match the others. Nothing disturbed in the house, and the items they took – an iPod, two BlackBerrys, a Picasso print, a clock in a dome ... very focused. No trashing.'

'I see,' I said. 'Well. Are you ready to start your employee interviews?'

'Just about,' Chris said. 'We had our first talks with management just before lunch.'

Julie cleared her throat. 'To put it mildly, that did not go well. They both treated us to tirades about how long they've been providing reliable services in this town. They say they have very stable staffs because they pay top dollar.'

'Which is still a pretty low dollar,' I said. 'I worked my way through school in service industries and I well remember the pay scale. And there's a certain level of turnover that they can never beat – some employees stay forever, but a lot of beginners hop from job to job. I do want to say, about Ole Aarsvold, that he's always struck me as the boss I'd want if I worked in yards and gardens.'

'Yeah, I like Ole too,' Chris said, 'but boy, I tell you, he's sure got his neck bowed right now.'

'What, is he giving you grief about sharing

personnel lists?'

'They both are. They're talking to their attorneys,' Chris said, 'about what they have to do.'

'Don't listen to any of that bullshit. I know what they have to do and so do they.' I gave them my close approximation of the Frank McCafferty stare that says, "Grow a hide!". Frank's stare alone can shrink an objection from a rant to a whimper – he doesn't have to say a cross word. I know I'm not there yet, but you have to practice when you get the chance. 'Tell them to quit tap-dancing,' I said, 'and hand over the damn lists.'

The two of them filed out of my office, and as I watched them go I admitted to myself that, while I was demanding a firm stance from Chris and Julie, I was letting Rosie Doyle stonewall me. I'd been given a direct order by the chief: to compensate for the shortage of staff and lack of training funds during the current emergency, insist that everybody share expertise and information. But I had given in to Rosie's reluctance to ask Bo for help – after Bo himself had offered it! I'd get one of those grow-a-hide looks myself if Frank found out.

I called Ray and asked him, 'Did Rosie tell you about the trouble she's having tracking the meth supplies from the house on Marvin

Street?'

'What? No.'

'Find her, will you, and the two of you come see me? I think it's time again,' I said, 'that we maximize our assets and check our priorities.'

'Oh, Jesus.' He was in my doorway, though, in three minutes, with a wire-haired, rebellious-looking Rosie by his side.

'Sit,' I said. 'Rosie, tell Ray what you told me this morning.' She didn't want to – she opened and closed her mouth a couple of times before anything came out, but I just kept nodding my head till she talked. I monitored her report, sending her back once when she left out the conversation with the Board of Health.

'Now, Ray,' I said when she finished, 'tell Rosie what your man Amos said in Phoenix, because she never heard any of that.'

'About the Mad Russians, you mean?'

'And the rumors about other cities … that stuff.' He told her about the kidnappings in Phoenix and the Walgreens concept as it related to thuggery in our time.

'OK,' I said, when he finished, 'have you both put that new information in the daily journal we're keeping?

With one voice, they said 'No.'

'And did you both read my report about

my lunch with the coroner?'

Again, like good children in school, together they said 'No'. And Ray said, 'But you told me about that, Jake.'

'But I didn't tell Rosie. See, we're already wrecking the new system. We all have to keep up this log and read it often, so we'll all know the same stuff!'

'Jake, we're too busy to keep sticking our heads in the computer,' Rosie said.

'It's quicker than coming in here and getting yelled at, isn't it? Listen to this.' I scrolled back till I found my notes about lunch with Pokey. As Rosie fidgeted and Ray sat wrapped in gloom, I read them Pokey's thoughts about the Cyrillic alphabet on the card and the lesions on the scalp of the deceased. 'Now then,' I said, 'which bright, enterprising detectives in this room think it's time they started working together and using the assets in front of their noses? Beginning with a call to Bo Dooley to get some advice about tracking those shipments, followed by another conversation with our man in Phoenix to see if he's found any more evidence of funny-talking gangs doing refined burglaries in other cities?'

Winnie was so late getting back from the pawnshop I was beginning to worry, but when she clattered in on her stumpy plat-form-soled stilettos she looked unconcern-ed.

'I stayed as long as I dared,' she said. 'Made up a lot of stuff about family-heir-loom jewelry ... Anybody interested in the going rates for jade? I've got a whole list.' She pulled it out of her purse and waved it like a flag. 'But our guys never showed.'

'Probably never found another house to hit after they got spooked into dropping the Anderson loot,' Kevin said.

'Well, that's it for you at that place,' I said. 'We've pushed our luck far enough.'

'I'm convinced the bad-suit guys are in on some of the burglaries at least,' Kevin said. 'But I don't have a shred of proof yet. And the only thing that connects them to the grow garage is a story by an admitted addict who's in treatment.'

'We need a picture or a recording,' Winnie said.

'Maybe somebody else,' I said, 'on another day.'

'The trouble is,' Kevin said, 'I don't have any more bright ideas for going proactive. I hate feeling like I'm just sitting here waiting for them to make a mistake.'

'We're not. We've got the employee line that Chris and Julie are following, and Rosie's

181

drug investigation, and Ray will get more from BCA soon. Something will pop. We'll make a list of all our loose ends in the morning and then prioritize, decide what to go after first.' He looked at me like he knew I was blowing smoke.

'Yeah. Well, I have to pull all that tape off myself, I better get going,' Winnie said. 'Is Rosie around to help me?'

'Yes. I'll call her,' Kevin said. Rosie came hustling down the hall toward us, spouting questions at Winnie, and the two of them disappeared into the Ladies. She didn't make eye contact with me then, nor a few minutes later when they came out and walked past my door together, deep in a conversation punctuated by gasps and chuckles. Their friendship seemed to be getting more solid every day. Rosie had never complained about working in a homicide crew with only men, but I could see it worked really well for her, now, to have another woman in the section.

I drove to Marvin Street past yards full of flowers blooming stupendously after the rain. The storm had been good news for roofers, too: several lawns were strewn with split shingles, and the crack of hammers sounded above the traffic noise. In Maxine's yard, where her old house had, amazingly, withstood the wind with hardly any damage, Nelly and a smaller girl who looked vaguely familiar were perched on the platform in the tree. Inside, Eddy was helping Maxine make meatloaf, and the two three-year-old girls, Brittany and Brianna, were competing fiercely to drape the most scarves and junk jewelry on to their dolls, out of a glorious mess they had spread on the floor.

'Hey,' I said. 'They look pretty fancy. Are they going to a party?'

'They're going to the *ball*.' Brianna said.

'Cinderella gotta stay home,' Brittany said, pointing to an abused-looking doll sitting naked on a doll bed.

'Too bad,' I said. 'Where's the ball?'

'At the ... at the...' Brittany said.

'Fairground,' Brianna said.

'Yeah, the fairground,' Brittany said, draping a fur stole around her doll's shoulders.

'Gonna meet the Prince, huh?'

'No, silly,' Brianna said, 'at the fairground you ride on the roly-coaster.'

As usual with Brianna, I stood corrected. I turned to Maxine and said, 'See you got a new client.'

'Mmm,' Maxine said, strangely noncommittal.

'Nelly *likes* her,' Eddy said, sarcastically.

'Nelly's being nice to her on her first day,

183

to help out,' Maxine said, 'which is pretty sweet of Nelly. You ready to add the oatmeal? One level cup.'

'I know, I know,' Eddy said. He was being a pill.

'Your little guy's still asleep, I think,' Maxine said, walking in with me.

As we leaned over the crib together, I asked her, 'Eddy doesn't care for the new addition to his harem?'

'Tiffany Funk. Her mother went into detox today, and her grandmother doesn't seem to be in any hurry to help out. So I said I'd take her for a while, but ... she's very shy and she kind of latched on to Nelly. So Eddy's nose is bent.'

'That's too bad. I wish I had a few minutes to talk to him, but I think I better get Ben on the road.'

'Absolutely,' Maxine said. 'Don't worry about Eddy. We're going to chop up an onion now, he can work his mad off on that.'

I'd always liked Eddy, though because of the trauma of living with an increasingly crazy father who finally destroyed the whole family in one day, he was more sensitive than most kids and still suffered from fear and survivors' guilt, and who knows what else. We used to have good little visits, though, as he healed up and began to talk. He liked to

184

play with my handcuffs and look at my shield.

I hadn't spent much time talking to him since Ben was born – I was always so busy now. And to be honest, now that I was a father, it made me uneasy to be reminded of Eddy's terrible childhood. I couldn't stand the thought of any of that bad stuff happening to Ben.

Now Maxine had another damaged child adding to the aura of waste and sorrow that was beginning to hang over her house. For a couple of guilty seconds I wished I had a babysitter with a happier clientele – as if Maxine was to blame for the trouble that sometimes got carried into her house. As if I wasn't lucky to have the best foster mother I ever had for a day-care provider. Shame on me!

I scooped up my son and hurried home with him, making grimly determined plans to give him a perfect life. About five miles east of Mirium, he lost faith in my ability to do that, and cried really hard the rest of the way.

Dead tired, that night I turned in right after Ben's last bottle and fell into a deep sleep that carried me far into REM country. In a recurring dream about prioritizing, I handed out lists of tasks to my crew. They all groaned in protest, but I insisted they get right on these jobs, and do them in the order I'd specified. Then something would happen that made me completely reshuffle the order in which the jobs had to be done, so I would trot around again, handing out new lists to increasingly hostile workstations. I was fighting off a direct challenge from Kevin – who was getting ready to throw a punch if I demanded one more change –when I woke up, sweating.

I lay still a few seconds letting my brain sort through layers of anger, frustration and guilt that it didn't have any further use for. When I emerged from the fog of sleep into real-time events, I heard a pair of owls trading owl bulletins in the trees outside my open window, and Ben, in his crib at the end of the bed, making the first, tentative snorts and whimpers of an infant about to demand a two o'clock snack. He had begun to sleep straight through some nights, but this was obviously not going to be one of them. The third sound I identified was the even breathing of Trudy, sleeping soundly beside me.

I slid out of bed, picked up Ben and a diaper, and beat it down to the kitchen, where I nuked a bottle while I changed him. As I sat down to feed him, I told myself not to get too comfortable – I was so tired I was afraid I'd fall asleep and drop him. Something about that combination – exhaustion plus determined alertness – put my brain into overdrive, and I began to have some quite interesting thoughts about the current crime wave in Rutherford. Ideas crowded around, waving for attention, each one pressing its claim to come first in the morning. I was too tired to write them down, though, or sort them in order of importance.

'And the trouble is,' I murmured into Ben's warm ear while I burped him, 'I'll probably forget all of this by morning.' He sighed as if he thought that was quite likely, and fell asleep on my shoulder.

I must have fallen asleep, too, between his crib and my side of the bed – I woke up cold, a little before six, with most of the covers down around my knees. But at least my memory hadn't failed me: all my ideas were still there, clamoring for attention.

'I don't see any way to prioritize them, though,' I told Ben over my shoulder as I drove to work. 'I think I'm just going to go after everything as fast as I can and see what shakes out.' He waved his fists and kicked against the restraints of his car seat, and then, to make sure I understood how completely he was on my side in this argument, he blew a bubble made out of his own spit.

EIGHT

Kevin was typing fast when I walked into his office. I waited for him to stop. When he didn't, I said, 'That Anderson kid, is he home from the hospital yet?'

'I don't know,' he said, without looking up. His voice implied that he didn't care and couldn't imagine why I'd expect him to. I fixed him with my best approximation of Chief McCafferty's Twin Blue Laser stare, not easy to do with brown eyes and a face that looks like the last item left on the shelf after a doorbuster sale. It must have been close enough, because when he realized I hadn't moved, he looked up, blinked, and said quickly, 'You want me to find out?'

'ASAP,' I said. 'And let me know.' I turned away, then turned back and added, 'If he's home, tell him to stay there.'

I walked quickly down the hall to Ray's office, stood in front of his desk, and said, in more collegial tone, 'I've been thinking about the Reddi-Kash pawnshop.'

He was reading something on his screen, but he swung his eyes up to me and said, 'So have I.'

'How long's it been at that location?'

'Forever. Long as I've been on the force. Eighteen years, going on nineteen.'

'And in all that time, have you ever had any trouble with it?'

'Never.'

'Neither have I.' I told him about my late-night conversations with Ike, back in the day. 'So I wonder, is Ike still there?'

'I don't know yet. I just started thinking about it. As soon as the Court House opens, I'm going to have Winnie call Records and find out if Reddi-Kash has changed hands.'

'Why Winnie?'

'I'm going to have her work in here with me today, making phone calls and bringing files up to date. That way she gets an over-view of everything, and just possibly I get caught up.'

'Sounds like a good plan,' I said. 'Now talk to me about the bad-suit guys.'

'OK. Wouldn't you like to sit down?'

'Not yet. If the bad-suit guys really are the ones Gloria called the Screamers, they are very bad guys indeed.'

'Agreed. And?'

'If they're also the burglars that assaulted

Ricky Anderson, maybe Mrs Anderson has a point about not letting them run around loose.'

'We haven't got anything to hold them on. And we haven't got them, either, as far as that goes. Although I guess that could probably be arranged if— Have you thought of a plausible excuse to pick them up?'

'No. But what I was thinking, if Darrell's dog matched them to the smell of something at the grow house, we could pick them up on the strength of that and Gloria Funk would ID them.'

He thought. 'Gloria didn't actually see them kill anybody.'

'So we might not get them on Murder One, but we could hang the drug rap on them for sure, and probably the assault on Ricky Anderson.'

For a moment he looked almost cheerful. Then he said, 'But we don't have anything of theirs for a dog to smell, do we?'

'I'm thinking there's a chance we could find something. Bring up that interview I did with Gloria Funk, will you? That first day.'

I didn't want to listen to the whole dismal thing again, so I fast-forwarded through as much of the weeping as I could. When I heard her say, 'Pete said if I didn't want to see it, I could leave,' I stopped and backed

190

up. And there it was, Gloria's face, swollen with weeping, saying, 'Helped themselves to anything in the refrigerator, too, Never even asked. And left their filthy socks and underwear all over the place, changed clothes wherever they happened to be standing.'

I hit the pause button and said, 'All that random undressing – isn't it possible there's a dirty sock or some skivvies lying around there somewhere?'

Ray said, 'BCA pretty well cleaned that place out, Jake.' He had a little gleam in his eye, though, like a coyote following a rabbit.

'If we got Gloria to come over and help us look—'

'Could we do that?' He licked his lips.

'Don't see why not. She's not in jail, she's in treatment. Right here in town.'

'But can they—? Are they allowed out?'

'Ask the judge,' I said. 'Explain that we just need her help for an hour.'

'OK. We'll do that and find out about the pawnshop, right away.'

'And speaking of the house, I was thinking maybe you could maximize one other thing for me.'

He didn't even flinch. 'What?'

'Andy Pitman.'

'What about him? He's out on a call right now, talking to a burglary victim who got cut in the window they broke getting into his house. Guy wants to make a case for reckless endangerment.'

'OK ... but remember when Andy was a COPS officer? A POP cop, I think we used to call it, when the program first started.'

'For sure. Andy was the COPS *FCber*-cop for a while. Wasn't he the one who cleaned up the Horton Tuck neighborhood?'

'Yes, he was.' Andy Pitman was a massive, ugly boy with crooked teeth when he joined the force. I've seen pictures in which he looks like a socially challenged hillbilly – you wonder how he made the cut. In the twenty years since, he's put on a lot of weight and neatened up a little. But his looks are irrelevant now, because he is legendary for his time as a COPS officer. COPS stands for Community Oriented Policing Services, and the year after we started it in Rutherford Andy took over the Horton Tuck neighborhood, a section centered on two blocks of rancid public housing that most cops entered only in pairs, with their holsters unsnapped. Walking a beat and knocking on doors, listening to retirees and housewives, and coming down hard on prostitutes and the local mopes, almost single-handedly, Andy saved a neighborhood that was sliding into slum status. He went on to train some of the officers who carry the program forward to this day.

Ham-handed, big-bellied, with a nose like a frozen beet, Andy's default expression has become a ferocious glare. He is on record for having uttered the longest string of profanity without repeats ever heard in the station locker room. But he's also famous for enlisting an entire neighborhood, including five hard little gang-bangers and a houseful of awesomely silent Somalis, in the effort that turned a trashed block into a sweet little city park with a soccer field.

I said, 'And didn't Andy help get that ordinance passed about absentee landlords?'

'I guess. So?'

'The homicide house – the grow garage.'

'Ah. You're right, he got a rule passed that says the landlord's responsible for what a renter does to a neighborhood. Got some nifty fines to make it stick, too.'

'Why don't you turn Andy loose on the house on Marvin Street? Have him find out who-where-when – all that good stuff – about the landlord. That could get us the name of the renter, right?'

'Plus a social security number or the lack of same. Yeah, Andy's an expert at putting the arm on absentee landlords – that was half the job in the area around Horton Tuck.'

'OK. And while Andy's there he could look for some wardrobe items the bad-suit guys left behind, couldn't he?' Beginning to look downright cheerful, Ray left a message on Andy's pager.

I turned to leave and collided with Kevin, who said, 'Ricky Anderson's resting comfortably in front of his Mommy's TV set, waiting for your call.'

'Cool,' I said. 'That his telephone number?' Then I remembered another idea from Ben's two o'clock feeding, and turned back. 'Ray, is Rosie around?'

'I'm right here,' she said, sticking her head out from behind Kevin.

'What are you doing?' I said. 'Stalking Ray's office?'

'I heard you over here and I came to ask questions.'

'In a minute. First I want to ask you some. You heard about the mugging that interrupted the burglary at the Anderson house?'

'Yeah, Winnie told me.'

'About how he got dope when he was supposedly on a tightly controlled vision quest for the good of his character?'

'She mentioned it. Do you need to know about that more than about the meth supplies?'

'Maybe not, but right now his story keeps

gnawing away at me. His father insists he sent him out clean – went through his luggage to be sure he had no controlled substances. But by some lucky chance Ricky supposedly leaned down from his horse, out there in the corn fields around Saint Charles, and found a dealer standing by the trail waiting to sell him some hemp. I have trouble imagining that. I'd like to know more specifics. How much did he pay? Was the weed in a baggie or a paper sack? How come he was carrying cash along? I thought one of the things they did on those quests was go out with nothing but the supplies in the wagon, so they'd have to fish and find roots and berries.'

'You're really curious about this transaction, hmm? And you want me to go ask him those questions?'

'Yes. I figure you've talked to enough dopers so you can probably tell when Ricky's telling the truth and when he's lying in his teeth, right?'

'Oh, yeah. I can do that.' She had begun to light up slowly, like a well-banked fire.

'Good, then do it. Go to the Anderson house, get Ricky to tell you the name of the group he rode out with and the exact location on the trail where that convenient cannabis salesman stood waiting. OK?'

'Totally OK,' Rosie said, in full blaze now. 'About time I had some fun.'

'Now, Kevin,' I took hold of his elbow, 'let's walk back to my office while you tell me how Chris and Julie are coming along with those employee lists.'

'Jake, it's eight fifteen and I've been doing your bidding ever since I got to work.'

'So you don't know?'

'No, but I bet if you'd get off my back for a couple of minutes I could find out.'

'Excellent. Call me as soon as you have that information. Today, if you think you can manage that.' I was being a pushy prick for a reason – I wanted him as far from his euphoric Monday morning mood as I could get him. Fighting mad if possible, seething to show everybody that he was smart and I was a mean unreasonable bastard. Because although Kevin Evjan relaxed is often a self-indulgent showboat, when he is in top fighting trim he can be keen as a blade. And that was the Kevin I needed now, a canny half-Norskie Mick with his teeth filed down to points.

My phone was blinking when I walked into my office. It rang while I was reaching to pick it up – and before I could say hello, Ray said 'Jake?'

'I just gave you a work list as long as my

arm. What more could you possibly want?'

'Clint just told me the most amazing thing – I don't know how he could have not noticed what we've all been working on all week, but somehow he didn't.'

'Ray, what the hell are you talking about?'

'Clint Maddox. Happened to be walking by my office and heard me asking Andy if he remembered the old guy who runs the pawnshop on the east side, and he stuck his head in and said Ike Kostas is his uncle.'

'Ike Kostas – the Reddi-Kash man? Is Clint Maddox's uncle? Now do you see what I mean about everybody reading the log? Bring him up here, right now.'

Clint Maddox came in a few seconds later with Ray, looking the way he always looks, sandy-haired, freckled and cheerful, like the Mayberry kid grown up. It would never in one million years have occurred to me to connect him with that sad, old Greek man with a handlebar mustache who used to perch on his dusty stool under a dim bulb on cold nights, trading gossip with me about neighborhood jerk-offs while dust motes drifted down from his crowded shelves. The American melting pot sometimes sweeps some very interesting genes under the rug.

I said, 'Sort this out for me. Ike Kostas is your mother's brother?'

'Her uncle. My great-uncle. His father came over steerage from Greece, went to Greektown in New York (don't ask me about it, I never been there!) hopped on the Greek grapevine – that's what he called it – and kept moving west from job to job till he got to Minnesota. Ike says Grandpa Kostas meant to keep going till he got to California but it was winter and he was cold so he got an indoor job, and by spring he'd met a girl. He used to have a little shoeshine stand in the Normandy Hotel, Ike says. Before my time, I don't remember.'

'OK. But Clint, you were right here on this floor all week and you never noticed that all the rest of us were talking about the Reddi-Kash pawnshop?'

'Funny, huh?' He enjoyed the joke. 'I was in my workspace working on the file for that latest gang fight at the Blue Moon Bar, and for once nobody bothered me.'

'We never bothered you because we were spinning our wheels at top speed trying to find out what's going on in that store. And now you say your uncle owns it?'

'Till about three months ago, when a guy came in the place and asked him what he'd take for it. Ike named a price and the stranger paid it, no questions asked. Just like that, in a couple of weeks, he was out of work for the first time in forty-four years. My Mom was so relieved. She's his only relative left in town, and she was afraid he was going to die in that shop. Are you OK, Jake?'

I realized I had started to count backward from a thousand and three by elevens. As I may have mentioned, math games help me control my impatience when people ramble on. I guess I look sort of brain-dead while I play them. I said, 'Is he still in town?'

'Uncle Ike? Far's I know.'

'Would you call him, please, and ask him to come in here? We need to ask him some questions about the new owner.'

'Sure. If I can figure out how to reach him.'

'I thought you said he was still—'

'He's living in somebody's RV till he decides ... He's always lived above the shop, see. Even when Aunt Gracie was alive, they lived upstairs and went downstairs to use that old wall phone by the desk. He's very frugal and old-fashioned, so I don't suppose he knows anything about cell phones or—' He saw me starting to zone out again and said quickly, 'I'll call my Mom. She'll know.'

'That would be just splendid, Clint. And will you repeat ten times "From now on I will read the log every day without fail!" while you wait for her to answer?'

He nodded sheepishly, got up, and went

out. I looked at Ray and said, 'Now you see why I want everybody to read the log?'

'Now you see what a pain in the ass it is to keep it up to date?'

'I always knew that. God, are we really going to catch a break?'

'I suppose that could happen, even to us. Not on the phone, though. Every number I've called today has asked me to leave a message.'

When he was gone, I finally answered my own message light. It was Lulu, the chief's secretary. She said, 'He wants to talk to you,' in a tone that suggested I should plan how quickly I could clean out my desk. But that's Lulu for you – she thinks cordiality is for wusses.

'Good!' I said. 'I want to talk to him, too.' After an empty silence I said, 'So put me through to him, will you?'

'Not on the phone,' she said. 'In here.' I hung up at once before she could assign me a time, like seventeen minutes from now, that would guarantee I waste seventeen minutes checking the clock. I walked briskly into his front office, strode past Lulu's space before she could block me, and stood in his doorway.

'Ah, Jake,' he said. 'Come in.' McCafferty looked his usual self, a big ex-jock fighting the fat of a hearty appetite, his desk covered with the piles of paper that computers never seem to make smaller. He wasn't scowling, but somebody must have stirred the pot a little, because he was kicking his desk and had a tell-tale pinkish look around the ears.

'About Mrs Anderson,' he said.

'She called you?'

'Boy, did she!'

I told him about the kid who got expelled from adventure camp and found his own escapade waiting for him at home. 'His mother thinks we shouldn't be letting these bad guys run around loose.' I repeated Ray's remark about the leash.

His grin lasted about two seconds. Then he bored in – where were we on this? I told him about our theory that the home invasions were melding with the homicide on Marvin Street. 'Naturally we haven't shared that theory with Mrs Anderson. But if she's indignant now, she may be even angrier soon, because Rosie Doyle is on her way out there to talk to Ricky.' I recited the Mama's Boy's hinky doping story.

'You think he's involved in this in some way?'

'I don't see how he could be, but this case is kind of viral … it seems to keep spreading. So I thought – well, Ray and I decided –

we'd better have Rosie go sniff around Ricky for a while, see what she thinks.' I slid that 'Ray and I' business in to reassure the chief that the chain of command was holding up, even in difficult times. Actually, I now realized I had assigned Rosie to that job without a thought for whether Ray liked the idea or not.

'OK,' the chief said. 'Keep me up to date, will you? I'd like to be prepared when Mrs Anderson attacks again.' Grateful that Ricky's Mama had decided to go right to the top and bedevil the chief, I agreed to replenish his ammo regularly, and was almost out of the office when he cleared his throat behind me and said, 'Oh, say?'

'Yes?' I half turned back.

'The Blue Moon Bar.'

'Clint's got the file. He's interviewing all the people involved. It's just the usual, I think, kids and alcohol and grudge fights.'

'I know, but keep an eye on it for me, will you? The City Council's fed up with that place, they've warned them twice and all they get is promises and more fights. They want us to let them know if we see signs of escalating violence there.' Not quite meeting my eyes, he added, 'They're counting on to us to let them know if we think they ought to pull the liquor license.'

'You bet,' I said, as politely as I could manage, and got out of his office without another word. Keeping an eye on the Blue Moon Bar was the textbook example of the axiom that shit runs downhill. The City Council wanted Frank to decide when it was time to cut off the liquor supply at a dreary no-class joint that was clinging to life by winking at teenagers' plainly fraudulent IDs. The place had attracted a faithful clientele of once and future high-school dropouts flashing hand signals and wearing gang colors. To work off testosterone and frustration at their low status, once or twice a night a couple of these groups formed up and beat the crap out of each other. Nights when the bar got lucky, they went out in the parking lot to do this. Then the neighbors complained, and the next day somebody from People Crimes had to go listen to kids with fat lips and black eyes explain that they were really innocent bystanders who got hit by a flying bottle. Ray had given the job of describing the latest fight at the Blue Moon to Clint Maddox, because it was his turn. It had not been a long or a complicated investigation – actually, you could cut and paste these things. Whoever you asked, it was somebody else who started the fight.

Frank, having no fondness for futile

chores, had just passed the responsibility for deciding when to drop the hammer on the Blue Moon down to me. I already had plenty of useful tasks on my list, so as soon as I left the chief's office I stopped by Ray's office and gave it to him, knowing very well that as soon as I was gone he would walk over to Clint's cubicle and ask him, in utter serious-ness, to keep an eye on the violence at the Blue Moon Bar and let him know if it was becoming a danger to the community. Clint was not born yesterday, and he had nobody to pass the job down to, so he cheerfully agreed to keep an eye on that situation for Ray.

So now, I thought, what next? I should probably have apologized to Ray for jumping the gun with Rosie – but he hadn't acted offended, so why bring it up? Let's see ... I wanted to talk to Darrell Betts. But he might be sleeping, as K-9 guys usually work nights, so I called his shift commander.

'Yeah, he worked until four this morning,' he said. 'But he'll be at the training session at Central School this afternoon from three to six. You can catch up with him there, if you want to.'

'If you're sure I won't interfere—'

'Nah. They take turns at practice. He'll have time to talk to you.'

Then Kevin was in my doorway, saying, 'Chris and Julie are here. Can you come over?'

They were sitting side by side, close together on two folding chairs, so they could share the same computer-generated lists. Julie's eyes had the beady gleam you sometimes see on raptors before they've had breakfast. Kevin had told me before, 'Julie's a wizard at sucking information out of meaningless lists.'

'I could see that for some reason Ole Aarsvold didn't want to give me a list of part-timers at the Yard & Garden store,' she said. 'He just handed me this short list of adult full-timers and said, "There you go," very proud of himself. I looked at the list and said, "What, no part-timers?" – because, you know, that kind of a service is very seasonal, they have peaks and valleys. But Ole said, "No, this work takes a lot of training, I use all professionals" – which is bullshit, because everybody knows that lawn care involves a lot of, you know, scut work. Wheelbarrows, raking, holes to dig and fill up ... All right, Jake, just a damn minute, will you? I'm trying to explain something.'

Julie knows me well so she can tell by my eyes when I'm starting to slide away. I was idly running through prime numbers and

205

had got as far as seventeen. I would have had to quit before long anyway, because they get big fast. 'I'm listening,' I said. 'Go ahead.'

'OK. We're just getting to the big brag here, so pay attention. Chris and I both have big yards, so we've poked around Ole's greenhouses enough to know that after school and Saturdays there'll be half a dozen kids out there wearing rubber boots and aprons, working their little butts off. But here's Ole insisting he only hires full-time. So I said, "Ole, your guys have planted a lot of trees in my yard and I know perfectly well they bring kids along to help, so stop flim-flamming and tell me who they are." Well, he just threw a hissy fit.'

'The more he protested, of course, the more we knew we had to get it,' Chris said. 'So I said, "Quit arguing or I'm going to get mean and subpoena your damn list, and if you make me really mad I'll charge you with obstructing justice." He squealed like a stuck pig but he finally wrote it out in longhand. The reason his payroll sheets don't show them is that he's been paying them cash, not taking out payroll deductions or anything. Two of his own boys and half a dozen others. They're all in the last two years in high school, he says, and he's trying to help them save up for college.'

'Not to mention paying them under scale,' Julie said. 'It's a two-way street.'

'I told him we were not working for the feds,' Chris said, 'and we had no interest in his little money games. But we had to get straight who works where so we can evaluate...' He waved his hand. 'I said something vague about the break-in problem, and Ole was so mortified about getting caught cheating the government that he forgot to be insulted about the implication they had something to do with burglaries.'

The two detectives looked almost as pleased with themselves as their boss did, a sight I rarely get to see. 'OK,' I said, 'so you got the list of part-timers from Aarsvold's. What about the home cleaning outfit, you satisfied you got all of them?'

'Oh, no trouble there,' Julie said. 'I mean, they were up in arms about getting investigated, but once they decided they had to hand over the lists, they ran the payroll right out from the computer, like there's nothing to hide.

'But then, as soon as we got out of there and compared lists,' Chris said, 'we saw that two of the kids are on both lists. One of them is Arnie Aarsvold,'

'They're working part-time in two places?'

I said. 'And going to school? Does Ole know that?'

'Don't think so,' Julie said. 'I thought I'd do a little more research before I talked to the boys. I already know they all go to the same school, Jefferson High, out there near the nursery.'

'Remind me of something,' I said. 'Didn't you say there were three houses on your list of home invasions where both services sometimes worked?'

'Um, yes.'

'And was the Anderson house one of them?'

'Yes. Who're you calling?'

'Rosie. I want her to ask Ricky what high school he attends.'

Her phone was busy. 'I'll get her in a minute,' I said. 'I'll let you know.'

'We'll be here for a while anyway,' Julie said. 'We're going to check both lists for priors. Also see if any names pop up on foreclosure lists or bankruptcy filings. What else?' she said, looking at Chris.

'Recent divorces, disaster stories.' They went away muttering like two evil crows. Experience has taught them how to look for stress points.

Rosie was almost back at the station by the time she answered my call. 'I was just coming in to ask you if you want me to stay on this,' she said. 'Because that kid's story about where he got his dope is ridiculous – but I couldn't press him much because his mother stayed right there, and pretty soon she was saying that's enough questions, he's got to rest now. So I wrote down the few answers he did give me with a straight face, and if you want me to, I'll start checking them now. I thought I'd start with the school counselor who recommended that quest.'

'Ah. So you know which school Ricky goes to?'

'Sure, Jefferson High. He hasn't been there for a couple of weeks, though. He was suspended for repeatedly sleeping in class and yelling at the teacher when she woke him up. That's what this trip was about – Ricky's been bad, he's about to get kicked out of school. Mom says that's the school's fault, by the way. They haven't challenged him enough. He falls asleep because he's bored.'

'Or stoned? OK, you're going to see the counselor and then—'

'Get the name of the company that runs those trips, and talk to the manager and the guide on the ride. If any of this takes me near where his dad works, I thought I might stop and talk to him. I gather he's been trying to get Ricky dealt with for some time.' She paused and said, 'This is what you want, right? I'm not sure it gets us any closer to the answer on the murder, but—'

'I'm not either but yes, stay with it. Let's collect all the lies people tell us today and see if they lead anywhere.'

'I can do that,' she said. 'No shortage of lies out here.'

I was beginning to think longingly about a cup of coffee, but as soon as I hung up Clint Maddox appeared in my doorway saying, 'Jake? I found my uncle.'

'Good!' I said, 'Can he come—'

Clint reached out a long arm and pulled Ike into the open doorway. He looked shy and older, a little unsure of himself now that he was not in his store where he had always been.

I stood up and shook his hand. He took a seat in front of my desk, shuffling in new white athletic shoes. I phoned Ray and Kevin, asked them to come in. While we waited, I asked Ike something inane about adjusting to a new routine. He squinted ironically and said, 'Forty-seven years I own-ed that place. And we hardly ever took a vacation. Raised two kids right there, above the store. I don't know if I'll ever ... Some days I wake up and see the sun already up, I get very excited, jump out of bed, and yell

"Oh God, I overslept!" Then I look around and realize I'm in an old RV in a vacant lot, by myself. It's over.' He shrugged, looking around. 'You're the boss now, Jake, huh? First colored cop in Rutherford, you did real good for yourself, didn't you?' There was no sting in the non-PC word the way Ike used it, beaming at me proudly. He was one of the merchants who gave me the respect due my uniform, back when I was still one of Frank McCafferty's braver experiments.

'I'm just the head of this section. Investigations. But yes, thanks, I'm happy with it.' I told him about my new baby and he beamed some more. Kevin and Ray came in, got introduced and found chairs. I moved a few pens around on my desk and coughed. 'Ike, we need to ask you about the people who bought your store.'

'Not people. Just one man.' His shrewd old eyes that had judged so many items and the hands that offered them, watched me now. 'He didn't buy the building, you know, I never owned that. Always rented from a real estate company in Des Moines. So it was just the inventory in the store he bought. He was representing a corporation, Riteway Incorporated. Took over the lease with the realtor, no trouble. Got the store license transferred to their name, no trouble. Seemed like all

211

went on greased wheels.'

'He paid you cash?'

'Didn't bring bills in a brown paper sack, if that's what you're thinking.' He smiled, but there was a little glint meant to say he wasn't born yesterday. 'Stood in my store and wrote a check – drawn on an account in my bank here in town, by the way. I deposited it in my account and it cleared in two days. When the money was there, I signed the bill of sale.'

'Did you hire an attorney?'

'When the man first started talking to me I said, "Don't we need a lawyer?" and he said, "I am the lawyer. But you can have your own, if you want." I talked it over with my son, he's a CPA. In a firm in Chicago. He looked the deal over, talked to his partners. He told me, "We can't see where there's any risk for you if you get the money up front like he says." So I went ahead.'

'You have copies of all the papers you both signed, don't you?'

'Sure. In the safety deposit box, locked up in the bank.' He watched me, waiting for the hammer to fall. 'You think there's something wrong with that man?'

'I don't know yet. You must have had some doubts yourself, didn't you?'

'Sure I did. Guy walks in off the street, offers to buy an old store in a bad location, pays the first price that's offered, you gotta wonder. This shop, back in the days with Gracie helping, we made a good living in it, sent two kids to college.'

'I remember you telling me – you didn't want them to run a pawnshop.'

'And they don't. As I mentioned just now, one's a CPA; and the younger one's a dentist. No evenings or weekends, and they make good money. Gracie and I had to work a lot harder, but we always put food on the table, good times and bad.

'But now, with eBay, all that other online stuff, ... and some of the new electronics, I don't know as much as I should. Business getting smaller every year. I was getting ready to just pack it in, you know, post a notice and in ninety days give whatever wasn't redeemed to the Salvation Army. With my social security and what I saved, I'd be OK. But this guy bought up the pledges at face value, even agreed to a few thousand for good will – more than I thought it was worth, but I asked and he paid it. It was found money.'

'You've been in business a long time,' I said. 'You ever found money before?'

He sighed. 'No.'

'Could you describe the man you dealt with?'

213

'Describe him?' His bushy old eyebrows went all the way up to his hairline. 'He was a middle-aged white man. What's to describe? Wore a suit and tie. Carried a briefcase.'

'Gold jewelry?'

'I never noticed any.'

'Ever see him in a running suit? A track suit, in a funny color?' Ike's expression as he listened to that question was answer enough.

'What's his name?'

'Uh ... Goldberg? No, Goldbloom.' He shrugged. 'I got it at the bank.'

I asked him to let me see the paperwork from the sale.

'Well now,' he said, 'I probably better talk to my son first, but I don't see why not.' He agreed to let me know as soon as possible. I thought he stood a little straighter as he walked out with Clint, and looked as if he enjoyed a little commotion. Maybe he shouldn't have sold the store just yet.

'Nice old guy,' Kevin said. 'But it's the new owner we're interested in, right?'

'More than interested,' I said, 'Getting downright fixated on Riteway Incorporated. Let me ask you both, does this begin to smell like a criminal enterprise? Well funded, well organized?'

'With tentacles,' Ray said. 'And growing fast.'

'Why would such an organization come to Rutherford?'

'Well now,' Kevin said, 'what's wrong with Rutherford?'

'Oh, please,' I said, 'this is not the Chamber of Commerce. What other cities did Amos talk to you about, Ray? Where they're seeing this particular cluster of quick skillful burglaries carried out by teams of foreign nationals?'

'San Francisco, Chicago. Three boroughs of New York City.'

'Right. And Amos is in Phoenix. Not as big as New York, but a big city compared to Rutherford.'

'See what you mean,' Ray said. 'Why would they come to Rutherford?'

Kevin said, 'Because they know where there's an old store they can buy very cheap and turn into a fence?'

'I can't believe they'd come just for that,' I said. 'But it does sound like they picked it out from a distance, doesn't it? Targeted it and came after it.'

'Yes,' Kevin said. 'OK, an old store and what else?'

'Maybe it's not complicated,' Ray said. 'Maybe it's just a handy fence next to a large metropolitan area like the Twin Cities.'

I said, 'The Twin Cities? Are they seeing

clusters of rapid home invasions in Minneapolis and Saint Paul?'

'Isn't it funny,' Ray said, 'that I never thought to ask?'

'And till right now I never thought to ask Amos,' I said, 'if he knows a Phoenix suburb that has an old pawnstore doing a lot of business all of a sudden.'

'Amos has never said so,' Ray said. 'I guess it's time for Winnie and me to make a lot more phone calls.'

'How's that working out for you? Having her for a helper?'

'Best idea I ever had. Like growing an extra head. I'm still pretending it's for her education – but really, I may never turn her loose. Everybody needs a Winnie.'

'That sounds like something to frame and put on a little stand on your desk.'

Finding out that Clint Maddox had worked on this floor for four days without hearing everybody around him talk about his uncle's store made me more determined than ever to get everybody on the same page. I carried a fistful of crude notes to LeeAnn's desk and, standing up and dodging constant traffic, dictated a quick and dirty version of the last two days' events. LeeAnn typed it all into the log at blazing speed. It wasn't pretty, but it was fresh information.

Rosie phoned in while I was there to tell me she'd seen the counselor. 'He says Ricky Anderson is strictly bad news in school, they're ready to expel him. This kid is in much more trouble than his mother's letting on. It sounds like he's been using for some time. I'm on my way now to interview the owner/guide of the adventure trip.'

'This is the man who sent the kid home?'

'Yes. Soon as I finish with him, I've got an appointment with Ricky's dad.'

As I hung up, I remembered I'd never told Chris and Julie that Ricky went to Jefferson School, too. I went across the hall to look for them, but Kevin said they'd gone to interview the manager of Home Cleaners. 'Julie saw something in one of those lists – she went out of here like her tail was on fire.'

NINE

'You about ready for lunch?' Ray asked me, at quarter to twelve.

'I'm sorry, Ray,' I said, 'I'm brown-bagging again.'

'I am too,' he said. 'Your Swedish stew the other day reminded me how much easier it is than going out.' The bag he held up was, in fact, immaculate white and cotton. And ironed? I kept sneaking peeks at it as we walked into the break room together.

'Cheaper too,' I said. 'I guess it might not seem so much easier if I made my own – but I have to confess, Trudy packs mine.'

'Yes, well.' He laid his flawless white bag sideways and pulled out a big roast beef sandwich, a dill pickle nicely wrapped in its own little bag, two paper napkins neatly folded, and an apple so shiny I could see my face in it. 'I been kind of lucky that way myself lately.'

I have been looking at Ray Bailey five days a week for eight years, so I guess I don't really see him at all any more, ordinarily. There's not much to ogle – he is what he is, never a handsome man and now passing forty, balding on top, his long, pale face as gaunt and gloomy as only a Bailey's can be. Reliable and hard-working, he is all you could ask in an able assistant, and I ask plenty. But his lunch today had the kind of square-corners elegance rarely seen in the hardscrabble break room, and never before in the hands of my plain-as-dirt bachelor lieutenant.

I subjected the individual to further scrutiny, as we say in police work. Didn't his near-sighted brown eyes show an unaccustomed sparkle behind his thick glasses? And the hair encircling his bald spot, wasn't it neat all the way around? Almost as if he had remembered to comb it. Also, there was a nice crease in his shirt sleeves that I didn't remember seeing there before, and the set of his shoulders gave off a new air of— Could it be optimism? Ray Bailey?

'Something's happened to you,' I said. 'What?'

He tried to look blasé, but blushed madly and grinned like a silly fool.

Then I saw it. 'You old dog. You and Cathy Niemeyer—'

'Finally made the deal. Yes.' Add a few zits,

his face would have looked right at home in Sophomore English class at Jefferson High.

'And you've already moved in?'

'What do you mean, already?' A touch of his usual cynicism finally reasserted itself. 'I've been running errands and chopping wood out there in Mantorville for two years. If anybody was keeping records, I'd probably be marked down as the slowest lover in the entire twenty-first century.'

'Slow but sure, huh?' We were both grinning inanely. 'Well, she had a lot of grieving to do.' The memory of that terrible day came back, sharp as a knife, the day Ray and I had to go tell her that her hero was dead.

'Yes. Maybe it sounds weird – well, it *is* weird – but that was what made me want her so much. When I saw how she cared about that guy. I watched her cry and I understood exactly what was missing from my life – nobody had ever cared for me like that. I been working for it ever since.'

'Looks like you've got it now all right. That's a killer lunch bag.'

'Isn't it? Look, it has my initials embroidered on the side.'

'Like there was probably going to be another one just like it in here?'

'Right. She has one of those sewing machines with a chip in it that thinks clearer than

220

I do. She sews on it like it's some kind of a sacrament. Bakes. Cans stuff out of the garden.' He rolled his eyes up. 'I'm going to get fat.'

'I'm happy for you, Ray.'

'Thanks. We're already saving up to get married.'

'So you'll be eating in here till you get enough for tuxedo rentals and flowers, huh? Does this mean I get to work you right through your lunch hour from now on?'

'Oh, listen, I wouldn't want to intrude on your quiet time.'

'Right. And of course I was just kidding. But as long as you're here, and we've talked about your social life about as much as I can stand, why don't you tell me how your phone calls went – you find any pawnshops in other states?'

'Not yet, but I started Amos looking for some. And his opposite number in Chicago says there's a weekend flea market he's had his eye on for some time. It seems to have too much new electronics gear. We're beginning to consider that they must do some kind of round-robin shipping to avoid selling the stolen goods close to home.'

'I bet they pay for the transportation costs by smuggling illegals in some of the boxes. Tell me, did Andy go to the grow house yet?'

'Yeah, he's over there. Soon as he's had a look around the place, he's going to the Court House to get everything they've got on the owner of the house.'

'And he'll look for leftover clothing while he's there?'

'I asked him to, yeah.'

'Did you make the deal for Gloria to come out and help?'

'The judge OK'd it, but the nurse at the detox center says she's too sick right now to go anywhere.' He sighed. 'I guess that's a rough road, meth withdrawal.'

'Yes. If Andy finds anything over there, I'd like to take it to Darrell Betts this afternoon and ask him about the possibility of a trace.'

'Oh? Hang on, I'll call Andy.' He held a conversation that made him wince and put down his pickle. Then he put the call on hold and turned toward me. 'He found a T-shirt behind the refrigerator that he says smells like horse sweat, and a very odd sock hanging from a rafter in the garage, up in the dark so BCA missed it. You want them?'

'Yeah. Ask him to drop them off before he goes to the Court House.'

I went back to work feeling that nice little undercurrent of excitement that you get when maybe your very own clever idea is going to work out.

Rosie breezed into my office, all pink and pleased with herself. She had just parted from Ricky Anderson's father, who was headed home to talk to his son. 'The guide from the nature trip told me Ricky pretended to be very surprised to find a friend sitting on the hood of his car at a crossroad about two miles out of town. Said Ricky's not a good actor. They held a brief powwow, Ricky and his friend, during which the guide believes a parcel changed hands. And after that, Ricky held up the ride twice for piss calls. During the lunch break he disappeared and kept everybody waiting fifteen minutes, wouldn't say where he'd been. He was on the nod all afternoon, nearly fell off his horse a couple of times. Right after dinner he disappeared again, was gone a long time, and wouldn't talk to anybody when he came back. So the next morning, when the group made its first rendezvous with the supply truck, the guide took away Ricky's horse and sent him home on the truck.'

'Did you make a plan with his dad?'

'Dad's going to get the friend's name and call me. After that, the three Andersons are going to map out Ricky's future. Naturally, Dad thinks he's going to check Ricky into rehab and put an end to all this nonsense.'

'Yeah.' We spared about thirty seconds for

the sad little silence that summarizes all we know about how to help an addict. 'You think he'll get the name?'

'Oh, yes. He's breathing fire.'

'OK,' I said, 'put it in the log, all you learned today, including the name Ricky Anderson gives up. Julie and Chris are on to something from the employee lists. Soon as they get back, we'll see if their information dovetails with yours.'

'Wouldn't that be sweet?' She paused in my doorway. 'I'm losing track. Is all this getting us any closer to the guys who killed the man in the grow garage?'

'Hell, Rosie,' Andy Pitman said, looming up suddenly in the space behind her, 'if those guys smell like these two pieces of shit' – he held up two plastic baggies, tagged and labeled – 'you don't want to get any closer than you are right now.'

I took Andy's baggies along in my pickup when I went to Central School, where Darrell's K-9 team was schooling dogs for their narcotics package. Two men in blue were in the parking lot with their dogs, encouraging them to sniff through a couple of cars. They told me Darrell was inside with the group that was searching cupboards in one of the home rooms. 'Just go through that door and follow the noise, you'll find them. We're the only ones in the building right now.'

I found them with no trouble, three men in the hall with big dogs on leashes. I didn't know any of them, so I showed my badge and asked for Darrell. 'He's inside there, working his dog right now,' the tallest one said.

'They said I might be able to talk to him between practices,' I said. 'You think that's possible?

'Sure. If you can wait a few minutes, he can talk to you when he's done.' He motioned toward the open doorway, where a fourth man and his dog were intently watching what was happening inside. 'You want to watch? It's kind of interesting how we do this.' He really wants me to see it, I thought – he had that same intense pride in the work that I had glimpsed before with Darrell.

'You can stand right there by Dan, he's our trainer,' the tall man said. The trainer had a shaved head as shiny as glazed porcelain.

I said, 'Hey Dan, I'm Jake,' and he shook my hand quickly before turning back to watch. Beyond him, inside the long room full of desks, Darrell was urging Sam to stick his big nose into cupboards and smell the chalk. Or no, he was showing him how much fun it was to find his white ball, his chew-toy

225

that he loved so much, and how he could find it again if he would just look into this ... Oh, look at this, the toy right here in this box, right alongside a packet of— Was that meth? He wasn't going to give meth to his dog, was he? But no, Sam didn't give a hoot about the meth, it was his precious chew-toy he was so glad to find. And Darrell was telling him again what a very good dog he was to find it.

'You see,' Dan said softly beside me, 'we play games with them, finding the ball and playing with it, but always with the narcotic next to it so they associate the smell of the narcotic with finding the ball. A little later we put the ball and the narcotic in a container with a plexiglass top and encourage him to scratch the lid to get the ball. After a while, he'll scratch wherever he smells the narcotic. It's all play to him,' Dan said. 'At first he always wins, he always gets to play with his ball. Later on, he only gets the ball when he finds the drug.'

'I notice he doesn't like to move as much in here.'

'It's the slippery floor. See how he hugs the wall?'

'Oh, yeah, I see that now.'

'They get used to it, but they never get to like it. These polished floors make them feel like they're on ice, they can't get a grip.'

'You need a lot of patience,' I said.

'Oh, yes,' he said, 'but the dogs are so rewarding. Being a K-9 officer is the best job in the department.'

'I believe Darrell mentioned that,' I said.

'I bet. He's really into it. Here he comes, his lesson's finished now. We got two more to go here, so you have a few minutes to talk, if you want.'

Darrell had to do his head-rubbing extravagant-admiration bit with the dog first, and then we went out and sat on the steps. I showed him the groaty underwear I'd brought along from the drug house where Sam had jumped on the man in the closet.

'I haven't broken the seal on these,' I said, 'But Andy assures me there's plenty to smell here. He said something like, "These undies ought to please the most discerning dog."'

'That sounds like our Andy.'

I told him my idea, that with Sam's help we could use these garments to track the bad-suit guys. 'I was thinking, maybe from one of the burglary sites to wherever they're living? Or from the pawnshop, or— Why are you shaking your head?'

'None of our dogs would be able to do that. All our dogs are air-scenting dogs. They can detect the odor of somebody who's hiding or running away, because it's carried on the breeze. I try to put Sam downwind of where I believe the person is, and if he detects a human smell blowing toward him he will follow it to its source.'

'You mean all those movies where the baying dogs track the escaped prisoners through the canebrake are baloney?'

'Those are bloodhounds. They track an odor with their noses to the ground. Sam's a German Shepherd. He'll find the things we train him to find by sniffing the air.' The dog had heard his name and turned his head toward Darrell, alert, like 'Yes? Was there something?' And Darrell, seeing that look, could not resist another gushing session of head-rubbing and telling the dog how superior he was to every other dog on earth. When he paused he said, 'A few German Shepherds do get trained to follow a scent on the ground, Jake, but we don't have any of them here. They have to work in an area where it's warm and damp, where a scent stays on the ground a long time. But you can find a guy who's hiding under the porch, can't you, boy?' I left them there, happy in mutual admiration, and carried my dumb idea back to the station, metaphorically with my tail between my legs.

I didn't have any time to mope about my

mistake, though, because my segment of the Minnesota justice system was running at top speed. I unlocked my door, put my briefcase on the console, and turned to see my doorway crowded with detectives, all with their mouths open, starting to talk. Every one of them wanted my undivided attention. 'I got a problem,' they all seemed to be saying. 'Help me figure this out. Where are we on this deal? Which way shall we jump?'

All except Andy, who as usual knew exactly where he was. I told him to talk first, because I knew he'd be quick – years on the police force had taught him always to do the next reasonable thing and not sweat about the small stuff, like sometimes being wrong. He told me quickly that the house with the grow garage was rented by Hogarth Peter Weber, using his social security number and driver's license.

'Who owns it?'

'Um ... a corporation named Riteway.'

'That's interesting.'

'Is it? They own that house and four other rental properties in Rutherford.'

'And the Reddi-Kash pawnshop?'

'Now where'd you get that idea? I know the guy that owns Reddi-Kash. Old Greek guy by the name of, uh, Ike something.'

'Kostas. Yes.' I told him about the recent

purchase.

'I'll be damned.' Andy did a series of facial contortions, each one uglier than the last, but they seemed to help him think. 'Now that really is interesting.'

'Isn't that what I just said?'

'OK, you two,' Kevin said, 'are you going to play Abbott and Costello all day or can I get a word in?'

'Get in as many as you want,' Andy said. 'I got other fish to fry.'

I said, 'Like finding out who owns the Riteway Corporation?'

'I know that. Sort of. Riteway is a wholly owned subsidiary of the Davilee Corporation.'

'Like that tells me a whole lot.'

'I know. All I've got on Davilee so far is an address in Chicago. Would you like me to follow this line of bullshit to its source?'

I smiled at him the way you smile at a clever child, and said 'Please.' He smiled back the way an ugly, aging, spavined seen-everything-twice detective smiles on the rare days when he is having fun, and left.

'OK, Rosie,' I said, to the outrage of Kevin Evjan, 'you're next. Did you get the name of Ricky Anderson's dope dealer?'

'Yes I did, and you are going to love it.' I gave her my don't-mess-with-me look and she said, quickly, 'Arnie Aarsvold.'

'Ole's son, no kidding?' Kevin said. 'Hey, I love that, too.'

'Bet you do,' Rosie said. 'You might want to take another look at all your recent burglaries. Maybe you can hang the whole cluster of clever ones on Ole.'

'Oh, come on,' I said. 'I don't believe that. Ole the tree planter? Hardest-working guy I know. Works right along with the newest of his grunts. What would he be doing mixed up with a gang of thieves?'

'Well, but didn't you just discover that this guy you think is so straight-arrow is paying his kids off the books? I'd say that's pretty unsavory.'

'Well, true. But it doesn't stink like the drug biz.'

Rosie said, 'Of course it's always possible his kids are in the life and he doesn't know it.'

'You think? Looks like he's got them right under his eye most of the time.'

'Ricky Anderson's dad has been watching Ricky pretty close, too, but he's been having a little party of his own.'

'You're right about that. Did you get a chance to talk to Ricky himself? Did you ask him who else was in on the deal?'

'Sure.' She shrugged. 'He says he doesn't

231

know.'

'You believe him?'

'He's a user, Jake. They all get very tricky. Maybe he doesn't know, or maybe he just isn't ready to give it up.'

'OK,' I said, 'you want to squeeze him some more? Or go to work on Arnie Aarsvold?'

'Oh, Arnie's definitely next.' She had that little irrepressible gleam, like an amateur poker player drawing to an inside straight. 'But maybe I should wait till Chris and Julie get back, huh? Didn't you say they were after something?'

'Something Julie saw in the lists,' Kevin said. 'That's what I came over here to tell you about, Jake. Julie made a chart of work hours and saw that two boys, Arnie Aarsvold and Tony Knowles, were listed for some of the same hours in both places.'

'Oho,' I said.

'You think?'

'Damn right. Tony Knowles is the son of the other owner, isn't he? Dave Knowles?'

'Come to think of it,' Kevin said, 'yes.' He blinked and wrinkled his nose. 'That sounds significant,' he said, 'but what does it mean?'

I said, 'It means both busy fathers have busy, busy sons who are up to something. And they might be up to it, whatever 'It' is, with their daddies. Right, guys?' I got about ten seconds' worth of nice warm rush out of that thought before my phone rang, and the chief said, 'Jake? Need to see you. Are Kevin and Ray nearby? Bring them along, too, will you? Please. Right away.'

'What is it?' Kevin asked me, walking over. 'You look a little agitated.'

'Because he was.' I didn't want to talk about it in the hall, approaching Lulu's desk. She waved us on without a word, which probably also meant something.

'I got another one of those heart-warming phone calls,' the chief said. 'I'll say this, as long as somebody wants to eat my liver every few minutes, at least I know you're all busy.'

'Who is it this time?' I asked him.

'Dave Knowles, from Home Cleaners. We shared a committee once on a Red Cross drive, and I guess he figures that gives him a friend in the department.' He let his large blue eyes wander across our chests, as if picking his targets. But his words were matter-of-fact. 'He wants me to tell my detectives to quit harassing him. He said, "I've been paying high taxes in this town for a good many years, I have a long list of satisfied customers who will gladly vouch for my integrity, and I'm not going to put up with being treated like a crook." He wants me to understand that my job is on the line.' Mc-Cafferty inspected our shirt-fronts some more. I began to think I must have dribbled some breakfast.

'We're not harassing him,' I said. 'Honest. Just doing what we gotta do.'

'Uh-huh. So what is it we gotta do? And for how much longer?'

We brought him up to speed, about Ricky Anderson's pusher and the double-up in hours that Julie and Chris went out to ask about.

'Remind me,' he said, 'does all this lead back to the homicide on Marvin Street eventually?'

'We're confident that it does, Chief. But we can't give out any of this information yet, because we're still not sure where the leak is.'

'I hear you,' McCafferty said. 'I got no problem taking the punishment as long as you think you're on the right track.'

'I'm very sure we are,' Ray said, in a suddenly take-charge voice. 'And I'd like to urge that we stay on it and hurry, because my man in Phoenix says he's seeing some signs that the Mad Russians they've been watching out there might be getting ready to wrap it up.'

'What?' I said. 'I hadn't heard that.'

'Because *I* just heard it,' Ray said. 'You

remember I told you we haven't matched their fingerprints on any database? Amos thinks the whole operation is a kind of gypsy band of illegals, moving from city to city, grabbing what they can and moving on. Looks like they're stockpiling cash, getting ready to set up a drug import business somewhere. They could go to ground if they feel threatened, though – they're not on anybody's lists. So we have to stay at arm's length till we're ready to grab them.'

'OK,' the chief said. He looked impressed by Ray's unusually firm stance. 'You got everything you need to follow this up?'

'For now,' Ray said. 'I've got all my lines out. We're ready to pounce as soon as they make one mistake. The trouble is, these rude savages are in some ways very sophisticated and careful. So far they haven't put a foot wrong.'

'Except for leaving one dead body lying around,' I said.

'Well, yes,' Ray said, 'that does seem impulsive and stupid. On the other hand we haven't been able to prove they did it, so far. So they're pretty good at covering their mistakes.'

'And all *I* need,' Kevin said, 'is for Julie and Chris to come back with the information they went out for. If they can figure out

235

which one of the home care specialists is doing the tip-offs, we can bring them in and pump out the rest of how this works. I'd like to pin down the local angle before we move on the transients.'

'I agree with that,' the chief said, 'it's the local guys I'd like to boil in oil. Especially,' he said, beginning to like the idea, 'if it should turn out that one of them is Dave Knowles.'

'I don't think we'll have the luxury of deciding who goes first,' I said. 'Once this starts to go, it's all going to go at once, Chief, and we have to be ready to grab those drifters before they get away.'

The argument about that went on and on, and eventually moved to my office. When Chris and Julie came up the stairs, Kevin stuck his head out and said, 'In here,' and they crowded in and perched on the console, looking tired and pissed off.

'I'm beginning to think they're *all* a pack of liars,' Julie said. 'I wish we could arrest everybody in both companies and lock them up till we get a straight story.'

'But which ones are lying about what?' Chris said. 'I can't seem to tell any more. At first they all looked like innocents with spades and brooms. Now they're all morphing into pushers and addicts. The longer I look, the worse they get.'

They took turns telling the story, of following Ole Aarsvold's big boots around the Yard & Garden store until he declared he'd told them everything he knew and didn't have time to talk any more. They told him they'd be back when all the kids were there, and went on to Home Cleaners. When they demanded that Dave Knowles explain the double scheduling, he insisted that the mistake could not be coming from his shop, and began to scoff at them for believing anything Ole Aarsvold said.

'Listen,' Knowles said, 'Ole pays his part-time kids off the books, haven't you caught on to that yet? He doesn't even know who's working there half the time. Those kids have just hoodwinked him into fattening their college funds with tax-free money.'

'But that isn't what the kids say,' Julie said. 'They say Ole told them when they started the cash-under-the-counter deal that he didn't want anybody thinking they were getting cheated. So he opened a special account book, kept it in a drawer and recorded their off-budget hours in it, said they could check it any time. And they all did, they got excited about how much faster the money added up if you kept it all and cheated Uncle Sam out of the taxes. They insist they never found a mistake. They've got this rationale about how kids shouldn't have to pay taxes till they're out of school, and are not at all apologetic about cheating the government. But they're very careful not to get cheated themselves.' She looked at Chris. 'Great bunch of kids, right?'

'Absolutely. Can't wait to hear their reasons for not paying taxes after they graduate.'

'What does Arnie say?'

'Arnie wasn't working today,' Julie said. 'Seems to me wherever we are now, that kid is not. We're going to have to bring him in here for questioning, I think.'

'But that younger Aarsvold kid, Axel,' Chris said, 'he's a go-getter like his Dad. He ram-rods the kid part of the operation, sees to it they deliver fair value per hours paid. Doesn't want Dad getting cheated either.' He chuckled. 'Everybody's got this twitch about fairness at the Yard & Garden store. Except they've decided Uncle Sam is a big sponge, so they'll gouge him every chance they get.'

'OK. But who's lying about the schedule?'

'I can't tell yet,' Julie said. 'Dave Knowles is so self-righteous he sounds like he's handing down stone tablets every time he opens his mouth. Never did anything wrong ever, never even thought about it. And brought his sons up to respect his values. Not a blemish on the whole family.'

'He's pretty cringe-worthy, all right,' Chris said. 'But we watched his payroll records come right out of his computer. We're getting what the government's getting, I'm convinced of that. But Jake, you know how easy it is to check somebody else's card in and out on the clock. And the older Aarsvold kid looks a little strung out, to me. Could he be into tipping off the burglars in return for his drug supply? Of course he could. But I don't know how we'll prove it unless we turn one of them.'

'Which we might do,' Julie said. 'After all, Rosie got Ricky Anderson to narc on his pal Arnie Aarsvold, didn't she? So why don't we see if we can get Arnie to turn in his pal Numbie Knowles? I meant to ask you,' she asked Chris, 'why do they all call that kid Numbie? Isn't his name Tony?'

Chris gave her a dumfounded look, opened and closed his mouth a couple of times, and finally said, 'It's short for "Numb Nuts", Julie. They claim he's no good with the girls.'

'Oh, for pity's sake!' Julie said, and got up and went to the rest room.

'Do you ever ask yourself what she's doing here?' Kevin asked Chris.

'Listen, Julie pulls her weight,' Chris said. 'She was raised by very conservative parents and she's in no hurry to change, that's all. Doesn't hurt to have somebody around here who's really nice, for a change.'

'Oh, yeah, so what am I?' Rosie said. 'Chopped liver?'

Aware that he had made a truly large gaffe, Chris unfurled his genius for the soothing answer. He leaned across his little pot belly, smiled into Rosie's eyes like the fondest of uncles, and said, 'No, Rosie, you're simply the smartest redhead of them all, aren't you?'

Rosie snorted and said, 'Yeah, sure.' But she wasn't really upset, she didn't want to be praised for good behavior anyway. She tossed her head another time or two, put the whole thing behind her, and asked him, 'So what do you think? Are the daddies in on it with the boys?'

I happened to glance at my watch then, and said, 'Aw, shit, it's five minutes after five.' Everybody looked at me as if I'd lost my mind.

Kevin said, 'Five after five on Thursdays *is* a bad time. I've always hated it myself.'

Speed-dialing Maxine's house and groping for my keys, I yelled, 'I'm late for my kid! Everybody out!'

Maxine was nice about my being late and helped all she could – she had Ben all wrapped up ready to go, and was waiting by the door when I got there. Ben was pretty decent about the schedule change, too, for the first few miles, just doing a little knuckle-gnawing and whimpering to remind me he was hungry. But he lost patience with me at about the halfway mark, and for the rest of the trip home he told me exactly what he thought of underperforming fathers who strap their offspring into car seats and leave them there to starve.

I believe I have mentioned that I find this distracting. My nerves were so frayed by my son's noisy protests that night, that as soon as Trudy took him out of my hands I muttered something about checking the potatoes, and went out in the yard. Then to make good on my own excuse for fleeing the house, I walked to the end of a row of potatoes, squatted down, and shook my head over the lacy patterns being gnawed into the leaves of several plants. No matter how hard I try, I kept saying to myself, I can't possibly do everything right. After a few minutes, as my pulse rate slowed down, I began to realize I wasn't talking about the potatoes.

'It's just what he has to do to get what he needs,' Trudy had said, more than once, about Ben's crying. She and I seemed destined never to be on the same page with this baby business. When she was first pregnant I had been over the moon with happiness, while she was worn down with morning sickness and worried about how deep in debt we were. Later, when the chemistry of pregnancy took her over and made her serene, I was bedeviled by worry for her safety and having bad dreams about a wolf. Before she went back to work she was hag-ridden with anxiety about leaving him, but I was certain Maxine would make it work. Now that Trudy was back in the swing of things, she was juggling job and baby like a champ, but I felt oppressed by the new schedule, crazy with worry that I could not do right by everybody and in grinding dread of the miserable trip home every afternoon.

And this case with all the fathers and sons in it was beginning to feel like a boa constrictor that I had been assigned to hold on to until it got around to strangling me. Given how long I'd been in police work, why did this particular crime cluster feel so personal?

Because, goddammit, I thought, it makes it so plain that you can try to do the right thing and still get everything wrong. Care for your son more than anybody else ever has and end up fighting him like an enemy. Want the best for your family so much you lose it all. What kind of a rotten, no-good, shitty deal is that?

A perverse mocking voice in my brain said, 'Welcome to parenthood, baby – the lifetime deal with no guarantees, the gift that keeps on taking.'

I realized I was holding on to the pasture fence with both hands, shaking one of the posts as hard as I could. My hands were sore when I let go, and my shoulders hurt. I took several long, deep breaths before I turned and walked into the house, where Ben was asleep in his downstairs crib and Trudy was stirring something red in a pan.

'That smells good,' I said. 'Spaghetti sauce?'

'Yes. You up to making a salad?

'Sure.' I took down two wine glasses, got out the Shiraz bottle, and poured us each a glass.

Trudy said, 'Thanks,' and took a sip, watching me over the glass. 'Is this where I'm supposed to ask you if you had a hard day?'

'No, I had the kind of a day cops have and that's fine with me. Can you tell me why I'm having such a hard time listening to Ben cry?'

'Ah. He punished you again, huh?'

'I know it's ridiculous.'

'No. Here.' She got out lettuce and trimmings. 'You chop and I'll talk. I think why it's so hard for you' – she stirred her pan again, tasted, and added things – 'is that you never had a family so you thought when you got one it would make life perfect. Isn't that right?'

'It *is* perfect,' I said. 'I've got everything I want.'

'Except it's driving you bananas. It's hard to leave your kind of a job right on the dot, and then after you break your butt to get over there and pick him up he rewards you by screaming at you all the way home. Some kind of perfect.'

'It's the same for you. You slave over a hot kettle of DNA all day and come home to a screaming baby and a husband who's half out of his gourd. How come you can take it? Is it your sturdy Swedish heritage?'

She laughed, a big, spontaneous gust of amusement that sounded so good it made my toes curl. 'My sturdy Swedish heritage? What a crock! I'm Trudy Hanson, remember? Raised by Ella, Our Lady of the Hairspray, dominatrix of many husbands? My sister Bonnie is the mother of the two kids from hell. Surely you haven't forgotten them? Or my Uncle Elmer, who wears women's clothes to family parties? He pretends it's a joke, and we all pretend to think it's funny. Stop and have a sip, we're not on a schedule now.' We stood by the sink, drinking wine a little too fast. She smiled at me and kissed me. 'I never, ever, at any time in my life I can remember, thought that having my own family would make life perfect.' She took another sip, leaned against the drainboard, and sighed. 'It's pretty good, though, isn't it? You and me and Ben, in our highly leveraged country place that I love so much.'

'It's better than good. It's wonderful, and I'll get used to the crying.'

She chuckled, a rich and satisfying sound. 'I think you just pronounced the epitaph for all human life.'

We had a good savory dinner then, and spent a half-hour in the garden in the last of the long dusk. We were working side by side along two rows, weeding carrots and beets, when Trudy sat back suddenly and said, 'Oh, I forgot to tell you, I found enough DNA on the knife handle to test.'

'Good for you,' I said. 'I guess it must be the dead man's blood. What does that prove?'

'That somebody stabbed him with his own

knife, cleaned it off carefully, and put it back in the holster.'

'Which means what? That these murderers are crafty, hard-hearted guys? I think I already shrewdly divined that.'

'You probably did. But if I find a second set of DNA in the mix, you might be able to shrewdly divine which crafty, hard-hearted guy it was.'

'Unless it was one of the bad-suit guys, who are not in any database.'

'Until you catch them, sweetheart,' she said. 'Then they will be.'

'You're a great little motivator, you know that?' I leaned across the growing vegetables and faster-growing weeds to give her a quick, warm kiss that somehow turned into a longer kiss that began to get downright hot. At one point Trudy said, 'Well, um, wait now...' and I said, 'I know, but...' And in a blurry minute or two we'd left a pile of weeds lying neatly by each row and were upstairs hurriedly wiping off our dusty knees so we wouldn't wreck the bed during R&R. We were both giggly and vague during Ben's ten o'clock bottle, and the weeds, for once, dried up and blew away on their own.

I slept hard all night and woke at dawn in a miserable sweat, trapped in a recurring dream in which Trudy kept saying, 'Ben's crying because you forgot to keep watching the pawnshop, Jake. It's the only way he's got to tell you that the bad-suit guys got away today, and it's all your fault.'

TEN

Enough with the guilt, I told myself in the shower. Be logical, as Mr Spock would say. You're the only father your son has got, so make up your mind you're good enough.

'We gotta bear down on this, my man,' I told Ben as I strapped him into the car seat. 'Your screaming and my guilt are not a good combination.' He was at the top of his game, waving his fists at the sunshine slanting across his blanket. He crooned a new little babble he was learning how to do, a small vocalization to let me know how much he enjoyed these fact-filled conversations we were having during morning trips.

'Actually guilt has it uses, though, if you think about it,' I told him as I drove to town. 'Like reminding me that I'm probably not the only dad in Rutherford who can't stand the thought of being in the wrong.' Ben waved and kicked to congratulate me on that insight.

The message light in my office was already

blinking. I debated three full seconds before I walked away from it. You never know what swamp lies steaming at the other end of a phone line, and I had some ideas I wanted to loft before wading into the slough.

Kevin was engaged in a landline conversation that sounded a lot too amusing for a police station. I listened politely for the few seconds it took to be sure the person on the line was female and was not a sworn officer. Then I placed my index finger an inch above the release bar of his phone, held up five fingers on the other hand, and said, 'Five seconds.' He said, 'Sweetie, may I call you back?' and hung up scowling at me, saying, 'What, for Christ's sake?'

'You still have the Krogstad twins today, right?'

'And half of next week. Yes. Why is that a burning question?'

'Any reason we can't put them to watching the pawnshop?'

'Um ... I don't think so. What's up?'

'I've got a feeling. Humor me.' I was pretty sure all the personnel at the pawnshop had recently changed, so I didn't care any more that Gary had once worked the neighborhood. I did worry about the fact that the twins were a little short on experience of surveillance in general – but they were the least essential people in the building, and since they were already scheduled to cycle back to patrol, they had the least interest in the cases we were investigating. I thought I'd ask Kevin to lecture them again about the need to fade into the background, and they could remember that much for one whole day.

I almost changed my mind when I saw them walk in. Gary was wearing ragged cut-offs and a Twins baseball cap, back to front. And Wally was even more outstanding, in lime-green pinstripe pants and a T-shirt that demanded, 'Get off my case.' They vibrated with last-days attitude. Their unlined sulky faces said, 'You already cut the orders to send us back on the street. What more can you do to us now?'

There was quite a bit, actually, that we could still do to them, but they knew we were busy and were not going to launch the long, tiresome procedure to get them fired over a little matter of stretching the dress code in the detective division.

They perked right up when they heard the assignment we had in mind for them. Spending the whole day sneaking around the pawnshop, phoning in weird reports of bizarre behavior, what could be more fun than that? Ironically, we now even liked their outfits – they might look defiant in Government Center, but they were just about right for hanging out on the south end of Broadway.

'I got groatier shoes than these in my locker, too,' Gary said, flashing his gap-toothed smile.

'Put 'em on,' I said. 'I don't know about using the old van, though. It seemed to me that maybe the bad-suit boys were getting a little curious about that vehicle the day I joined you down there. You got anything else you could use?'

'Our dad's got a pickup for his fifth wheel, we might be able to get that,' Gary said.

'Oh, hell, it's quicker if you use my old fishing car,' Kevin said. 'It's a '69 Jeep Wagoneer and the body's so rusted out you can see through it anywhere, but the motor's still reliable and it'll look right at home in front of a pawnshop.' He slid the key off his ring and held it out to Wally, telling him, 'Now remember, you've only got two or three gallons of gas and it does about twelve miles to the gallon, so don't take any side trips.' Then he called home to tell his mother not to call 911 when she saw 'two skinny kids dressed like juvenile delinquents' driving it out of the back yard.

Before he let them go he shook a long forefinger at them, saying, 'The men you're watching for are presumed armed and dangerous. Wear your body armor. Don't argue, put them on and keep them on. And if you see these guys, don't try to pick them up yourselves. You see them, you call me. At once, hear?'

They gave him Christmas-morning smiles and were out of there like a shot. Watching them go, Kevin said, 'Sometimes this job scares the piss out of me.'

'Tell me about it,' I said. Fear is not a good thing to discuss out loud in a police station, so after that conversation I needed comfort and went looking for a jolt of caffeine. In the break room, I stood with my mug in my hand watching Andy Pitman pouring the whole bottom third of a pot into an immense styrofoam cup. When I cleared my throat he looked around, saw my cup, and said, 'Oh, do you want some of this?' and quickly put the pot down.

I poured the skimpy half-cup he'd left me. 'Actually, you are just the man I wanted to see,' I said. 'In my office.'

He executed a tiny, delicate shrug that lifted dozens of pounds of gristle a quarter of an inch and allowed the whole mass to settle again. 'Lead on,' he said.

When I closed my door he said, 'If you lock it, I'm calling my Mom.'

'My heart is pure,' I said. 'Now don't amuse me any more, we got a gutbuster day going here. How far did you get with the search for the people involved in Riteway?'

'Riteway is owned by the Davilee Corporation. I told you that, right? Davilee was incorporated a little over a year ago. It's a real-estate management firm that appears to be entirely owned by its board of directors. Meets twice a year, issues a report, the officers sign it, all pretty ho-hum. All of Davilee's properties are in Chicago. Riteway is a newer corporation, set up about six months ago. All it does is buy and manage properties in Rutherford.'

'You got any names?'

'Far as I can see Riteway is run by an executive secretary in Chicago, looks like a paid hand. She signs the checks and files the papers. In Rutherford, she has a contract with a company to clean and maintain the buildings, execute the rental contracts, and hand out the keys. Aaaannnd,' he said with a little flourish, 'that company is Home Cleaners.'

'Ah.'

'Yeah. It gets more interesting, too. The president of the Davilee Corporation, the man who signs the checks, is Lee Kostas.'

'Lee Kostas? Would he by any chance be

"my son the CPA"?'

'Bingo! He grew up over the pawnshop, I remember him now. He went to Jefferson High, we played intramural football against each other.'

'So that's the Lee part of Davilee?'

'Uh-huh.'

'And the Davi part? Oh, I can guess where this is going.'

'Yup. The vice president of the corporation is David Knowles.'

I once owned a cat I called Tweedy because his calico pattern looked liked orange tweed. Days he mostly slept, but at night he turned into a fearless hunter, and he liked to bring home small creatures, mice and voles and gophers, to arrange neatly on the kitchen step for my approval. Looking at me now the way Tweedy used to look up from the bottom step in the morning, Andy said, 'Does it seem to you the mischief is starting to stack up into neat piles?'

'It does,' I said, 'although it doesn't quite get us where we need to go, does it? Owning houses is not a crime, per se.'

'No.' His large, doughy face looked a little disappointed. 'But it gives us probable cause to search the shop, doesn't it? All this cozy business – Lee Kostas and David Knowles, the houses and the shop, and the crazy

Russians?'

'Yes, it does. And I'm not saying ... You did a great job, Andy!' His face had just reminded me that, even more than the taste of fresh mouse, what Tweedy wanted on those long-ago mornings was praise for his skill as a predator. Ray and I recruited Andy into investigations to get the benefit of his long experience policing the toughest streets in town. We got an undeserved bonus when the lumpy terror of the gang wars turned out to be a closet geek. He loves to travel the Internet in search of, oh, the title of a book you read in grade school about a Shetland pony, or a current street map of the ancient city of Tashkent, or the name of the winner at the Viola Gopher Count in 1938. Or the names of the officers of a Chicago corporation named Davilee. And he's like Darrell's dog – it's all a wonderful game to him, so he never tires of it. Wanting to show appreciation for his efforts, I smiled and asked him, 'Have you told Kevin yet?'

'No.' Watching me, he gulped a huge swallow of coffee out of his monster cup. 'You're not satisfied yet. What don't you like?'

'How many of the boys at those two companies are in on it? It's pretty hard to tell, isn't it? We know they're playing cute games with the IRS and some of them are padding their work hours, but do they all know they're in bed with major-league crime?' I drank some coffee. Mine tasted bitter. 'Does Ole know?' Andy shrugged. 'And how about' – I finally said what was really bothering me – 'Ike Kostas?'

'You mean did he know all along that his son was buying his shop to help some un-registered aliens get into the drug biz? How would I know that?'

'If Ike didn't know,' I said, 'if he wasn't part of the plan, don't you think it's inter-esting that his lying deceitful son saw to it that he got paid top dollar for the shop? And even got a few thousand extra for good will?'

'In a minute,' Andy said, turning moody, 'you're going to start saying nobody's all bad, huh?'

'God no. I was about to say this changes almost everything we were going to do today. How about that?' I laughed out loud, sud-denly, realizing how perfectly this morning was imitating yesterday morning's dream. 'We have to reprioritize all our tasks! Let's go find Ray and Kevin.'

By now, Andy was giving me the look you usually get from the man guessing your weight at the county fair. But he came along with me to Kevin's office, where Julie Rider sat frowning as she flipped through her notebook. She was reviewing her notes from yesterday's investigations.

'I feel like those high-school brats bamboozled me some way,' she said. 'I've been over and over this and I still can't decide which ones are lying to me.'

'Let Andy help you,' I said. Her dissatisfied frown smoothed out as he told her about the Davilee Corporation.

'So Knowles is in on it?' Julie looked dubious. 'He is so not my idea of a gang-banger. Does this mean Yard & Garden's off the hook?'

'We don't know that,' I said. 'Maybe Ole, but I think you should take another look at Arnie. And the whole Anderson household, eventually. How could Ricky Anderson get so far into weed and meth, and nobody else in the house have a clue?'

'You're right,' Julie said, 'his parents would have to be blind and deaf.'

'Or up to something themselves,' I said. 'Why don't you copy Ray's and Rosie's notes from those interviews? See if you can see anything obvious. If not, maybe you and Chris ought to go back out there and interview them yourselves. One at a time.'

'Better still,' Kevin said, 'maybe we should bring them in here and do that in an inter-

257

view room. Sometimes the presence of re-cording equipment concentrates the mind...'

'What's this?' he said, looking up. 'Every-body run out of work at once?' Five of his detectives were standing in his doorway, with Chris Deaver in the lead.

'We've got to bag the employee list thing for now, Kevin,' Chris said. 'We just got a fresh cluster. Three new break-ins, all re-ported in the last half-hour.'

'OK,' Kevin jumped up. 'Everybody in here, let's figure out the teams. I think we're going to have to pull the Krogstads off the pawnshop, Jake,' he said to my back as I walked out.

'No,' I turned back into his crowded office, bullied my way to the head of the line. 'Absolutely not! Soon as you get your teams going on this cluster of crimes, I want you to call those Krogstad boys and tell them they are not to leave that shop unwatched for a single minute. Tell them, if they have some problem that can't be solved by taking turns, call us and we'll get them some help. My gut is telling me we're going to see a lot of action at that shop before this day is over.'

'You think the burglars will bring in the merch that fast?'

'If Ray's contact in Phoenix is right, they might be headed there right now. And this

258

could be our last chance to nab them. Amos thinks they're getting ready to wrap it up out there – and if they are, these guys might be getting ready to go, too.'

'Go where?'

'I don't know, that's the point!'

'So now all of a sudden you're ready to grab the whole outfit?'

'With all this probable cause Andy just found,' – Andy tucked in his shirt and looked modest – 'I think we've got all we need. Gloria will be well enough to testify soon, and with her help we can hang all those drugs from the grow house on them. Any luck, we'll catch them with some loot today. So yeah.'

'So we'll still wait a while on the shop?'

'I'd like to try to take the bad-suit guys first. The shop can't go anyplace, let's get the thieves put away first ... I'm going to negotiate with the chief for an Emergency Response Unit standing by all day today, ready to go whenever we spot them.'

'OK!' Kevin said. 'Hear that, guys? Gangbusters today.'

'Yeah. I'll go tell Ray. Soon as you've made your assignments, Kevin, come over and we'll set it up with the ERU. We need everything ready to go as soon as we see the first bad suit.' I crossed the hall thinking hard.

Before we talked to the ERU guys, I should alert Rosie and Winnie. We might need them to back up the Krogstads ... What else?

My phone was still blinking. The message said I should call Rosie Doyle. I called her and said, 'How'd you know I wanted to talk to you next?'

'Next after what? Never mind, I'm the one that wants to talk to *you*. Urgently.'

'You forget where my office is? All right then.' As soon as I hung up, I heard a drum-beat of click-clicking heels along the hall, too much noise even for Rosie Doyle. Then the springy red curls and the shiny black braids stood side by side in my doorway, the faces underneath not smiling at all. Oh shit, I thought, there *was* a swamp at the end of that line.

'We did something brilliant,' Rosie said.

'Or anyway clever,' Winnie said. 'Even if it was kind of an accident.'

'Don't waste time sugar-coating it,' I said. 'Just tell me what you did and I'll try to fix it.'

'Boy, feel the love,' Rosie said. 'Isn't that gratifying?' They exchanged a quick uneasy glance.

I ground my teeth. 'Tell me what you did.'

'Last night after work...' Rosie started.

'...we decided to eat Chinese,' Winnie said.

I looked at Rosie, raised my eyebrows. She blushed and looked at her shoes.

She wasn't eating with Bo any more, and she didn't want to talk about it. Fine with me, I didn't have time to hear it. I said, 'Will one of you just please say it?'

'We were paying our bill at the counter at Wong's,' Winnie said, 'when I looked out the glass door and saw two of the bad-suit guys walk by. Right there on the sidewalk, a few feet away.'

'Walking on the sidewalk,' I said. 'How low can they sink?'

Rosie made that same little shushing motion at me that she'd made before at Kevin's back. 'Winnie nudged me and whispered, "There they go!" And I knew right away they were the guys you'd all been talking about. The velour and the gold chains, aren't they just too good to be true?! I watched them get into their flashy SUV—'

'That Escalade we saw in front of the shop,' Winnie said.

'Winnie was looking at them like a kid at a Christmas doll,' Rosie said. Her cheeks were bright, remembering. 'And I said, "Would you like to see where they go?"'

'You didn't tail them!' I said. 'Tell me you didn't follow those weird thugs in an RPD Crown Vic that any grandmother could spot without her reading glasses!'

'Well, no,' Rosie said. 'We had two cars.'

'That's why we knew it would work,' Winnie said.

'And it did,' Rosie said. She grinned like the old, let-'er-rip Rosie that hadn't been much in evidence lately. 'We stayed on our cells and traded being the tail every couple of blocks, talked each other through the turns, and – omigod, Jake! – you would have been so proud of us. That Escalade is beyond easy to follow in traffic.'

'Flaming-red body the size of a house,' Winnie said, 'spinner hubcaps, and stainless-steel door-sill plates. Surprised they don't have a beacon on it.'

'They've probably got that on order,' Rosie said. They traded quick delighted glances.

'So you followed them in two Crown Vics,' I said. 'Even more subtle!'

'No, I was driving my own car,' Winnie said. 'See, I promised to lend it to my brother while his was in the shop, and he was going to run me home later so I could—' She saw me starting to puff up and muttered, 'Never mind.'

'Your car,' I said. 'That cuddly little yellow Volks that I'd recognize across town in a heavy fog?'

'Maybe you would recognize it, but they

wouldn't,' Rosie said. 'I'm telling you it worked, Jake.'

'I'll bet it worked for them, too,' I said. 'They probably let you follow them around until they were sure they recognized Winnie from the store.'

'I don't believe so,' Winnie said. 'If they knew I was there, why would they let us follow them home?'

'Do what?' I stood up so fast they both jumped. Kevin walked in my door at that moment and found us all standing there, staring at each other and breathing hard. He stayed in the doorway, silent for once, and watched us with great interest. I said, 'You followed them home?' They nodded. 'How do you know?'

'Know what?' Rosie said.

'That they were home.'

'They both got out and went into the house,' Rosie said. 'Isn't that what you do when you go home?'

I sat back down and said, 'I'll be god-damn'd.'

Kevin said, 'Soon as you got time, Jake ... The reports are starting to come in from the first responders, you might want to come over.'

I consulted the ceiling light for a couple of seconds, trying to remember which first responders I had ever been interested in.

Kevin said gently, 'Three burglaries...'

'Of course,' I said. 'I'll be there in a few minutes.'

When he was gone I said, 'Where is this house?'

'On Benton between Fifth and Sixth Street – that nice retro area of fifties ramblers, detached garages, big old yards with hollyhocks and lilacs. I was so surprised to see them going into a sweet place like that. I thought all those houses were owner occupied. How do you suppose they even found it?'

'What's the address?'

'523 Southwest Benton Avenue.'

I wrote it down. 'Did they put their car in the garage?'

'No. Parked in front of it, in the driveway, like they intended to go out again soon.'

'But they walked right in the front door?'

'Side door. Next to the garage. Kitchen door, I'd guess.'

'All right,' I said. 'I don't want either one of you within ten blocks of that place till we find out if those guys are really living there, you hear me?' Rosie opened her mouth to say something indignant, but I saw it coming and cut her off. 'Yes, OK, what you did was very clever. Brilliant, even. You both get A in sleuthing. It was also impulsive and potentially dangerous. Can you be absolutely certain those guys didn't spot you?'

'Come on,' Rosie said, 'you know that's impossible.'

'That's right, it is. And these are almost certainly the drug dealers who killed that man in the garage, are you really ready to bump chests with guys like that?'

'I'm as ready as anybody else is,' she said, turning red. 'Why are you treating me like a girl?'

'I'm not. I'm treating you like a good investigator who made an error in judgment. You know we don't go off the reservation and do things like that without backup.'

'It was a sudden opportunity—'

'Yes. And knowing where they live, if they actually do live there, might turn out to be ... convenient. But now everything's starting to break wide open – as of today almost this whole department is on this case. What if you blew it for everybody?'

'What do you mean, break wide open?' Right away, she lost interest in the lecture, she just wanted to know about the action.

'We got a new cluster of break-ins. We're hoping to pick up the bad-suit guys today, and take down the store.'

'Ah,' Rosie said. 'How about my boy Arnie

Aarsvold?'

'He's not going anywhere. If you're right about him, we'll get him later. For now, don't talk to him or any of the Aarsvolds. Or Knowleses or Andersons, if you can help it. Stay away from anybody connected with this case. Both of you, try not to do anything that will make all this work go to waste. OK?'

'All we did,' Rosie said, 'was try to help catch the bad guys. And I think we did, too.'

'I hope so,' I said. 'We need to put surveillance on that house right away, but it can't be either one of you. And most of Kevin's crew is out on calls right now. Maybe Clint ... I'll see. You two can go back to whatever you were doing before you came in here. What was that?'

'Working for Ray,' Winnie said.

'Good. Go back to his office, and tell him I need him to come up here as soon as he can. What about you, Rosie?'

'I *was* trying to get an interview with Arnie Aarsvold,' Rosie said. 'But I can't seem to find him. Not at work, not at school. He's seventeen, where else could he be?'

'Almost anywhere, I'm starting to think. But don't look for him any more, I don't want him to know we're on his tail. I might need you two to describe the bad-suit guys to everybody that's going to be looking for

266

them soon, so don't go anyplace. You hear what I'm saying? Do not stick your faces out the front door of this building today without checking with me first.'

When they were gone, I walked across to Kevin's office. In a congested space where two phones and a steady stream of people competed for his attention, I perched in a corner and absorbed information from the overflow.

'Nobody's hurt,' he told me during a lull. 'All three of these burglaries follow the pattern we've been seeing – in and out, focused and clean. Except—' his phones sprang to life again and I had to wait. He had sent Julie and Chris to the McMansion on the northeast side that had the biggest losses to report, and Julie was calling to tell him they would probably be out there all day and would need tech support to help with fingerprints and photos.

'Jesus, three flat-screen TVs!' he said, when he could talk. 'And a whole fucking bin full of brand-new designer bags and shoes. Lady just got back from a New York shopping spree. She said to Julie, "Really, it's as if somebody knew where I'd been!" You think? She probably told every single person she talked to since she got back.'

'What's the exception?' I asked him.

'The what?'

'You said "nobody hurt except", and then you had to answer another phone.'

'Oh. Nobody got hurt because, as usual, nobody was home when they broke in. But the older couple on Benton took it hard when they came home from a trip this morning and found all their best heirlooms gone. They both got sort of shocky and had to be taken to Emergency. Word now is that they're going to be fine, though.'

'Where on Benton?' It wasn't, of course ... It couldn't possibly be ... But then Kevin read off the address, and it was the house Rosie and Winnie had followed the thieves to, where they watched them enter. It was 523 Benton Avenue Southwest, the nice fifties rambler with the hollyhocks and lilacs, where all the best heirlooms were gone.

ELEVEN

By ten o'clock the Emergency Response Unit was assembled and standing by. In Rutherford, it's made up of the best-trained members who happen to be on duty that day. In a force as lean as ours was getting, there was no question of keeping five men hanging around equipment lockers waiting for a call – so 'standing by' meant they were going about their regular duties but monitoring their radios every minute. ERU guys are always looking for practice, though, so I knew when we summoned them they would blaze right into the station and gear up fast.

The Krogstad twins radioed in to say they had found an excellent spot for surveillance. 'We're in the parking lot by the sushi place, pulled up close to the fence,' Gary said. 'We got a good view of the front of Reddi-Kash, but from inside the store they can't even see us. Even out in front of the store, you'd have to know we were here to spot us. We're surrounded by a hedge and some garbage cans.'

'You're not blocking an alley, are you?' Kevin asked them. He was not exuding the confidence we like to see in our leaders of men. Because he hates to fire people, he'd steeled himself for the awful task of demoting the Krogstads by persuading himself that they were not as bright and special as he'd originally believed. As they grew angrier at him over the loss of a rating, he grew surer he had never liked them at all. Now that they were almost ready to go back on the street, he was close to believing they should not be outside without keepers.

I couldn't see that he had anything to worry about. OK, they had overdone casual Friday a tad – but now that they were on assignment they were fully engaged, their reports were incisive and precise.

Admittedly they had very little to report, at first. The lights were on in the store, they said. Now the squinty manager had unlocked the front door, swept the sidewalk, and rolled out the awning. And he was doing business as usual – a scabby loser from last night's bar scene brought in a boombox and left a few minutes later tucking a few pitiful dollars into his jeans.

Listening to this trivia made Ray and Kevin almost too hyper to sit still. I stayed in my office and tried to work, but I was almost as distracted as they were. It still seemed a little unbelievable to me that the burglary cases we'd been working on for weeks were going to merge with last Friday's murder and land the culprits in our laps. I had worked for this day as hard as anybody and I wanted it to happen – but so much could go wrong.

We all had our desk radios turned up high enough to hear the traffic in the cars, so everybody was talking louder than usual, which by itself made us all jumpy and irritable. I was answering emails, making short terse phone calls, and shuffling the most routine paperwork while I monitored the scanner.

When the duty sergeant called to tell me there had been another call-out of several cars to stop a brawl at the Blue Moon Bar last night, I was inclined to blow that nuisance off until Monday. But then the sergeant said, 'And the chief asked me to remind you we need to stay on top of that situation.' So now Frank was checking on my work? I would have liked to get seriously annoyed, but I didn't have time.

Be it recorded, I walked the Blue Moon call down to Ray's office first. But he had stepped out for something. So before the Blue Moon Bar ate a hole in my gut, I went

271

along to Maddox's cubicle, where I knew this job would end up anyway, and gave the call to him. I asked him to interview the complainants, talk to management, and come back with his assessment of the situation before close of business. Maddox, having nobody below him in the pecking order and being much too cool to waste his breath pointing out the futility of this assignment, tucked his notebook in his pants and walked out of the building whistling a merry tune.

I left a message about Maddox on Ray's tape, and went back and listened as Wally, on the radio from the pawnshop, described the scabby loser walking away with his dollars. In the background as he talked, I heard Gary answer his cell phone in the middle of the first buzz, speaking softly and then a little louder. Then Gary was on the radio, saying, 'Houston, we got a problem!'

Dispatch, not at all amused, said, 'What problem?'

'Our Mom just— Wait, I'll call Kevin on the phone.' I went across the hall to Kevin's office, hearing his phone ring. When I got there Kevin was listening to Gary, saying, 'Mm,' and 'Mm-hmm,' into the phone. After a minute he said, 'Hang up, I'll call you back.' He put the phone down and said, 'Ray?' and Ray, who was walking past in the

272

hall, turned and came in.

'The Krogstads' father just had a heart attack at work,' Kevin said. 'He's in an ambulance on his way to Emergency. One of the twins has to go help their mother, she doesn't drive. Gary says he'll stay, but we need to get a replacement for Wally over there, driving a car Wally can take to go home.' He looked at the two of us. 'Who, though? Every one of my detectives is out on a call.'

Ray said, 'Clint Maddox.'

'I just sent him to the Blue Moon Bar,' I said, not meeting his eyes. 'I left a message on your phone.'

He swallowed once and said, 'Andy, then.'

'I was hoping,' I said, 'to keep him in reserve in case we start some rough stuff.'

'Yeah, you got a point there,' Ray said. 'Well ... Winnie's had a little too much exposure over there already, right? So it's gotta be Rosie.' He looked at me. 'You think she got made when she and Winnie followed those guys?'

'No ... not really. Anyway she's just going to sit in a car. Rosie'll do fine. Let's get her going.'

Kevin gave her the bullet-proof-vest lecture and the call-the-minute-you-see-them lecture, and Rosie said 'Yeah, yeah, yeah'

273

and headed for the stairs. But a memory had floated to the surface of my brain, and just before she started down I said, 'Whoa. Hold up a minute.'

I went over and stood beside her and said, 'Used to be a funny little alley in back of that store. It's narrow and not used much any more, but why don't you take a look before you hand over the car – see if you can drive along there and look at the back of the store?'

'You're really having a worm about that place today, aren't you?'

'Don't hang around too long and let them spot you,' I said, and right away I knew I'd said one thing too many. Her eyes flashed and she tossed her red curls and stomped down the stairs. She is the daughter, niece and sister of cops, and she hates any implication that she is not as good at the job as any one of them. Well, rightly so – but she makes me anxious sometimes, she's a little bolder than I want her to be.

She did exactly what I asked her to do that day, though, circling the block discreetly before she pulled into the lot by the restaurant. Then she turned over the keys of her unmarked squad car to Wally Krogstad, got in beside Gary on the old quilt that had taken the place of seat cushions in the ancient Jeep, and phoned Kevin.

He came trotting across the hall to my office, carrying the phone in his hand, with a little film of excited sweat on his upper lip. 'Rosie says that before she gave Wally the car she drove down the alley behind the Reddi-Kash, and there's an eighteen-wheeler in there by the back door. And those big cars we saw out in front before, they're in there too.'

I reached, and he handed me the phone. I said, 'You think they're loading up?'

'Yeah, the back door of the store is open, and the van's ramp is down. It's happening right now.'

'Good job! This is just what we've been waiting for. Now listen, the two of you sit tight there, you hear? I need you to be eyes and ears. Tell Gary to stay on the radio. You hang up and call me back in five minutes on my own cell. I'm going to ask Dispatch to send the ERU team now. Stay in that car, Rosie.'

'All *right*, I *hear* you,' she said, and hung up.

'Get Ray,' I told Kevin and called the duty sergeant to deploy the ERU squad. They were patrolling in their own sectors, but none of those Type-A guys wanted to take a chance on missing this gig, so they had not

275

gone any farther off than they had to. Within minutes, they were all in the basement gearing up. Helmeted, encased in body armor and carrying shields and a steel ram, they'd gladly take down anything I asked. I've seen the mess they can make, so I don't ask often – but when you need them, there is nothing like an Emergency Response Unit to lift the spirits of an overworked investigator.

They got ready fast, but not fast enough to suit Ray and Kevin, who spent the intervening minutes jittering over the radio, picking the brains of their detectives on stake-out and agonizing over the chance that the clever burglars we'd been chasing all week might still somehow slip away. When they'd had all the anxiety they could stand, they dispatched Andy Pitman to check on the action around the store. 'Just stay on the radio and circle the block,' they said. 'Let us know if you see them around there.'

Andy clipped his Glock on to his belt and clattered out. Ray and Kevin were in my office by then, so we could all listen to the radio together. After three or four minutes of traffic stops and a fender-bender, the monotone voice of the 911 operator came on the radio. She said, 'Car 41, see the man at the Reddi-Kash pawnshop.' She gave the address and added, 'He's reporting an armed robbery in progress.'

Vince Greeley's voice came back from Car 41 saying, 'Copy, the Reddi-Kash.' And a second later Andy identified himself and said, 'I've got it too. I'm right there.'

My phone rang. I said, 'Yeah?' and Rosie said, 'Greeley's just pulled up, and now Pitman's here too. They're both headed into the store right now.' I heard the sirens below me, as the ERU boiled out of the basement in three cars. They can make a silent approach when they need to – but when, as now, noise works to clear their way, they make plenty of it and flash a dazzling array of strobes. They went screaming south on Broadway, stalling traffic for a couple of blocks around them as they went.

I opened my mouth to tell Rosie the team was on its way, but she cut me off, saying, 'Gunshots in the store! Two ... no, three ... now three more together...'

Then Greeley's voice on the radio, a little blurred, said, 'This is Greeley, ten-ninety-nine—'

There was silence on the phone and then a little thud. I said, 'Rosie?'

After a couple of seconds, Gary Krogstad said, on the phone, 'Rosie's out and running toward the store. Shall I go help her or—'

'No, Gary! Listen! The ERU's almost

277

there. Stay on the phone and tell us what's happening.'

'OK.' He breathed hard, three times. Involuntarily, the three of us began to adjust our breathing to his, but then he rapped out, 'There's an officer down, did you hear that? OK ... now the ERU's pulling up to the store, they're all running toward the store ... they just threw in the flash-bang ... now they're all going in.'

'Where's Rosie?' I asked him.

'She's behind them. She only made it half-way before they got here, so now she's stopped, she's waiting to see ... Oh, wait, a car's coming out from behind the store. I guess that's what she heard. It's ... uh ... the Ford Excursion. She's firing at it! But they're not stopping, she hit the cornerpost of the wind-shield but it bounced right off ... they're turning, I gotta get out to see this, just a min—' In a few seconds he was on the radio, giving the license number and requesting that officers in the area pursue and stop the Ford Excursion heading north on Broadway.

As soon as he stopped talking, one of the ERU team – Burnap's voice I thought – came on the radio giving the address of the store and saying, 'Start meds code three, I have an officer down here.'

Then Gary picked up the phone again and

said in my ear, 'There's gunfire out in back of the store now, Jake, and I can see a big ... it's an ABC Movers van ... coming out. Rosie's behind one of the ERU cars, she's firing at it but it's going right on...' He was back on the radio then, calling in the license number of the van, also reporting that it was turning north on Broadway. 'Driver's talking on a cell. I think them three vehicles are all talking to each other.' There was more transmission from other cars, very fast, including two that were following the van, reporting it turning west on Twelfth Street.

Gary's voice came right in behind them, giving the license number and description of the Escalade. 'Big red SUV, pulling out of the parking lot behind the store. Need cars to follow...' But then he was back on the phone to me, saying, 'Jake, there's a man running alongside the Escalade on the far side. Rosie can't see him but he's coming right at Rosie and the driver's firing at her now, she's down behind the car, I gotta go—'

Then there was silence on the phone, silence on the radio. An eternity of silence went by before Gary's breathless voice on the radio reported that the two men from the Escalade had disarmed Rosie Doyle and were driving away with her in the back of their vehicle. 'They're going east on Twenty-First Street. I am in pursuit,' he said. 'Looks like they might be turning north on Third Avenue ... Yes, turning north on Third Avenue now. I'm in pursuit. Request assistance from all cars. We must apprehend, repeat, must apprehend this vehicle! Suspects took Doyle, they have Rosie Doyle on board.'

I still have the impression that the lights dimmed while he talked. In the dusk of our dread, Ray and Kevin and I stared open-mouthed at each other, momentarily brain-dead as we listened to the hellish screaming of sirens all over town.

Hanenburger called in at once to say he was joining the chase. He was part of the ERU, had detached and come over from the store, was passing the Jeep and gaining on the Escalade.

As Hanenburger reported them crossing Sixteenth Street, Car 45, one of the two squads chasing the ABC van, came on and said they had been joined by a third car coming south on Highway Fifty-Two and were 'making a box around the suspect vehicle in the parking lot at Apache Mall.' We could hear all their sirens wailing as he spoke, then there was a brief silence until he came back on to say, 'Car 45, we have the suspects from the ABC van in custody.' The sirens seemed to go right on screaming, though. Some of them stopped a minute later when a matter-of-fact transmission from Car 62 reported the Ford Excursion had been stopped on Southwest Sixth Street and the driver was in custody.

We had three thumbs in the air in my office now, Kevin was muttering praise words about the 'home team'. Then Hanenburger was reporting the Escalade 'blowing through the red light on Twelfth Street, we're going to try to follow.' It's a big major intersection on what's called the Beltline, a busy bypass around the edge of town. The commotion from all this chasing, you'd think, should have alerted every driver in town to pull over, but there's always somebody listening to tunes on the radio and blissfully unaware.

Three of these dreamers piled up, with a great screaming of brakes and blaring of horns, in front of the crossing when the Escalade parade rolled through. And it *was* a parade by now, the Escalade being chased by an ERU car driven by Al Hanenburger, a squad driven by somebody he called Buzz, and Gary lumbering along behind in the old Jeep, determined to stay in the game and rescue Rosie.

The squads were faster and much more

maneuverable than the Escalade, which had bulk and power but turned like a tank. What the Cadillac's driver had going for him, though, was utter disregard for anybody's life but his own. He just bombed through everything, going flat out, counting on the vehicle's size to clear out the laggards. But the officers following him had to dodge around bikers and seniors, and housewives sporting little signs saying 'Baby on Board'. Knowing that, Dispatch broke in to say gravely that they should consider abandoning the chase.

Hanenburger answered with a firm 'Negative, an officer's life is in danger here.'

He was back on his radio frequently from then on, calling out his position – he had taken charge of the pursuit. Anton Hruska, on patrol west of Broadway, announced that he was now heading east below the golf course and would intersect the chase at Broadway. Ruskie was driving one of the three new squads, we all knew, and it had a pretty good kick. I heard Al say quickly, to the car beside him, 'Buzz, drop back and let Ruskie up here.' The black-and-white beside him said, 'Ten-four,' and faded back. And in a minute, Ruskie said quietly 'Coming right up behind you, Al' and then 'Sixth Street coming up', and I heard Al say something fast, like 'Try at (blank) Center.' I thought what he was trying to do was position Ruskie alongside the Escalade and a little ahead, get Buzz right behind him, and make a box with Hanenburger in back of the Escalade, so they could force the Escalade left into the Government Center parking lot.

It might have worked, too. I'll never know. I ran downstairs fast, clipping my Glock on my belt as I pushed out the door, and got ready to help if I could. I was ten feet into the parking lot when the cars screamed past, the Escalade still a car's length ahead on the right, Ruskie and Buzz coming up fast in the left-hand lane. Plainly, the plan had been to make for the Civic Center parking lot on the other side of the street. I stood watching, knowing Ruskie's car had the poop to over- take the Escalade and get enough ahead of it in time if the traffic would get out of his way. But I saw there was a minivan dithering just ahead.

Ray and Kevin rolled up by my left elbow in an unmarked squad. I jumped in back. Winnie opened the door on the other side and climbed in too. I yelled, 'Winnie, what?'

She yelled back, 'They've got Rosie!' Which seemed a bit unnecessary, why would we all be out there otherwise? But Winnie had been in the ladies or somewhere and

283

had only just heard it. Anyway, Ray had already released the brake and was rolling forward, so she was coming along whether I liked it or not. Inside Government Center, Dispatch was suggesting again that the pursuit should be abandoned. Hanenburger said back, 'Negative, they've got Rosie!' and we heard no more about that idea.

Ahead of us, as we all streamed on to Civic Center Drive, we could see the Escalade pulling away from the other cars. Failing to catch it in time to mousetrap it as they'd hoped, the police vehicles were all hitting their brakes and slowing down now, because they knew about the sudden rise over the railroad tracks just ahead.

The Escalade's driver did not know about it, or he forgot. He hit that tremendous speed bump doing almost eighty miles an hour, and went airborne. It was a gleaming spectacle for a heart-stopping few seconds, the crimson behemoth throwing off sparks, wheel-well debris, and a spectacularly spinning hub cap, which clattered down the street bouncing off half a dozen vehicles before it collapsed in the gutter. The Escalade came back to earth with a sound like trains colliding.

Its expensive suspension system delivered, though. The car held together and went on, a little slower, till the driver's vision cleared. Then he began to pick up speed again along Silver Lake Drive, but Al Hanenburger, seeing his chance to catch up after he'd crossed the tracks, sped up in the right-hand lane, and Hruska stayed with him on the left.

At the north end of the lake, the roadway turns sharply west, heading toward North Broadway, and as Hanenburger traversed this tight curve at a speed he had never attempted before, we could see him start to skid. All his iron discipline kicked in at that moment, and he turned, as he had always been taught to do, in the direction of the skid.

But he didn't have any wiggle room at all. There was an asphalt walkway on his immediate right, then a wire-and-metal-pole fence enclosing twenty feet of fluttering goose-repelling tinfoil on wires, and beyond that another fence like the first one. When Hanenburger turned in the direction of the skid he crashed right through all of it, trailing a silvery kite's tail of miscellaneous metal. It slowed his momentum just enough to allow him a flat entry into the shallow water of the lake, with maximum splash.

His air bags did not deploy, so his head hit the steering wheel and broke his nose. But he fought his way out of his sinking vehicle, and came wading toward shore as we passed him. Soaked and muddy and bleeding from the nose, he shed bits of wire, tinfoil and watercress as he walked. His lips were moving. I knew I didn't want to hear what he had to say.

The Escalade negotiated the turn successfully, but as soon as it straightened out and picked up speed again it encountered another hazard unique to the area – a single file of Canada geese strolling across the road. Local mascots their whole lives, they were so accustomed to doting humans who looked out for them that it never occurred to them to check traffic or hurry.

The Escalade blasted through the goose parade almost as fast as it had hit the speed bump. The geese got alarmed in the last five seconds and tried to take off. There was a wet *thock!* as two of them hit the windshield, scattering blood, feathers and goose parts across the SUV and the roadway. The big car's driver roared on, but now he and his passenger were seeing the world through two fist-size holes in a feathery red tracery of shattered windshield.

As I watched all the cars turn north on Broadway, I realized that from as far behind as we were we would never overtake them. I leaned forward and said, 'Ray, we're never going to catch up in this old bucket. But listen, they're not going to go to Lake City, right? They've got connections in the Twin Cities – they're most likely to go there.'

Ray said, 'Yeah, so?'

'So take Elton Hills Drive to West River Parkway and we'll catch them at the pistol range.' I said it fast and just in time. Ray screeched into the turn at the last possible second. We all swallowed hard as the car tilted before it settled back down on to all four wheels. I watched the Escalade and its followers roar away to our right, where North Broadway turned back into Highway Sixty-Three.

Ray said softly, 'Good call,' and then we all sat through an anxious, silent interval of hoping I'd guessed right about where the bad guys would go. But as we approached the last long curve that would turn toward Thirty-Seventh Street, we heard Ruskie saying 'Turning west now toward River Parkway' and we all exhaled. The Escalade came in sight soon after, blazing fast along the southern perimeter of the pistol range. Trailing some smoke now, but still with plenty of speed, it turned north and screamed along the parkway, doing close to ninety in the right-hand lane. Ruskie was in the left-hand lane, coming up on the SUV's flank and gaining a foot now and then. Ray found an opening between the second squad and Kevin's Jeep, and we were finally part of the parade.

Then we all said at once, 'Hey!' Because ahead of us, at the northernmost edge of the pistol range, Bo Dooley had just pulled calmly on to the roadway on his old Harley, and tucked in right behind the Escalade. As he explained later, he had been shooting some qualifying rounds on the pistol range. Like most of us, he wore both foam earplugs and Optimum 3 earmuffs – so he was really in his bubble, and when he took off the protection and heard a great wailing of sirens in town he was immediately curious. He turned on his radio just in time to hear Dispatch suggesting the chase be abandoned, and the answering protest, 'They've got Rosie!' He turned up the sound and strained to hear every word then. When he realized the pursuit was coming his way, he got on his bike and got ready.

North of the pistol range, the Zumbro River makes a long curve that carries it close under the steep bank on the right-hand side of the road. And apparently the two men in the Escalade were beginning to feel less certain about their chances of escape, because as we passed the mink farm on our left, with its myriad furry creatures nibbling happily, oblivious to looming disasters including their own, the window on the passenger side of the SUV slid down, and a velour-covered arm began throwing things into the river. Two guns flew through the air first, and then a number of tightly wrapped packages. Kevin said softly, 'Just look at that wretched waste of weed.'

Ahead of us, Bo had begun to make a series of swooping dodges, left and right, across the rear of the Escalade, as if he were deciding which side to go around.

'What's he doing?' Ray said. 'He can't possibly have speed enough to pass.'

'Maybe not,' I said, 'but that must be distracting as hell for the driver ahead.'

Maybe so, but the Escalade's driver, out of town now and seeing a nearly empty road ahead, must have thought his chance to outrun the pack had improved. He appeared to put the pedal to the metal in some newly motivated way, and began pulling a little away from Hruska. He just had to shake this pesky little bike rider, he must have been thinking, and he'd be gone.

But he didn't know the road as well as we all did, and maybe his eyes stayed on the motorcycle in his rear-view mirror a second too long. Where the road turned sharply left on to Fifty-Fifth Street, and the river, completing its ox-bow, flowed west alongside it, the big car had too much speed – or the driver's reflexes were getting tired. For whatever reason, he blew the turn.

Roaring straight ahead off the roadway, he passed a sign, brown with white lettering, that read 'Entering Controlled Hunting Zone' and began to climb the bank as nimbly as a goat. A few feet farther up the slope, a similar sign had once stood, but it had been hit from behind, perhaps by a snowmobile last winter riding the top of a drift. Now the sign was gone, but the metal post remained, bent forward toward the road. The Escalade hit it straight on. It pierced the windshield somewhere on the passenger side, got scooped out of the loose soil of the bank, and carried right along.

The bank wasn't steep, so the Escalade didn't lose much speed going up. It seemed to me that maybe the driver froze at the wheel, that he'd reacted to one too many things and lost his flexibility for a few seconds, so he kept his foot on the gas instead of hitting the brake. However it happened, he kept on going, simply flew off the top and disappeared, headed down toward nine feet of dirt-laden Zumbro River. We couldn't see the plunge from where we were, but we saw the top of his mighty splash.

Bo drove a few feet up the bank, and when the bike slowed he jumped off and dropped it in the dirt. He ran fast up the rest of the slope and then he, too, disappeared. All the rest of us made the quickest job we could of pulling cars off the road and getting out – there was a rattling prattle of talk from car radios and slamming doors, and then we were all running up the bank. All except Kevin, who yelled, 'I've got some flotation gear in my Jeep – help me get it, Ray,' and the two of them headed for his old fishing car.

I'd thought most of the damage from my gunshot wound last winter was healed, but my left leg turned to jelly on the climb, so everybody passed me. I was so disgustingly out of shape, I had to stop at the top for a breather.

I had a spectacular view of the Escalade from there. It had dropped nose first and entered the river at a steep angle. And that thing was so damn long, even with its front bumper firmly buried in the mud, it still had six or seven feet of rear end protruding above the stream. It had twisted a little to the right during its fall, or the bottom had subsided more under the right front tire, so the passenger side was deeper in the water than the driver's side.

The river bank was noisy with scrambling policemen and treacherously sliding rocks. Bo was already at the water's edge, wading in. As I started down the bank, the water reached his chest, and he began to swim.

Winnie passed everybody on the climb up, and then bombed straight down to the river at iron-woman speed. When she reached the water she ran right into it without a pause, and in a few seconds she was swimming, too. By the time Bo reached the Escalade, Winnie was right behind him.

Realizing that we didn't know who might come out of the vehicle, or what shape they'd be in, I limped down the bank yelling, 'Wait, the rest of you wait! Cover the car till we see if anybody comes out!' At first they said, 'What? What's he saying?' But as they reached the water and thought about jumping in, they also began to think about the need for backup with dry weapons. By the time I reached them, they were all bracing on the wet sand with their Glocks in their hands.

'OK, Gary and I can cover it now,' I said when I reached them. 'You watch the passenger side, Gary, I'll take the driver. The rest of you, make a line, huh? As far out as you can get without swimming, so you're ready to help when they bring her out.' They stacked their weapons behind me and edged into the water. Ruskie was tallest; he reached a wobbly foothold about halfway to the car.

Bo swam alongside the upstream side of the vehicle till he could reach the roof rack, where he hoisted himself aboard in one gutsy move that must have taken all the muscle he had. The car settled a little more to the right but held its place in the current, and he pulled himself quickly along the sloping roof, toward the rear end.

When his head was out over the tailgate he looked in through the glass panel at the top, nodded down at Winnie in the water, and tried the door handle with no success. He twisted sideways and pulled his radio out of its holster. His arm rose once, twice, three times. Pieces flew off the radio but a hole appeared in the middle of the glass. He dragged himself upright on to the roof rack, managed to sit up at a crazy angle, and kicked with the heel of his boot until the hole was bigger.

I heard him tell Winnie, who was clinging to the wheel well on the high side, 'Wait right there.' He reached in through the shattered glass, groped till he found the handle, and turned the latch. He said 'Now!' and jumped into the water with blood streaming from his arm. Winnie pushed up and the liftgate rose.

The two of them scrambled into the open back hatch.

Ray and Kevin, panting hard, came crashing down the bank carrying line and floats. They plunged into the stream, which by now was so mud-filled it afforded no visibility at all. Clinging to the floats, they had plenty of buoyancy but poor forward momentum – they had to kick furiously, with their eyes above water, just to avoid floating away. The men in the water began to grab them and push them forward toward the car, and they paid out line as they went.

There was a little rocking motion at the open hatch, and then Bo and Winnie crouched in the opening, holding Rosie between them. She had her eyes open, she seemed to be having some trouble standing but I could see she was talking – didn't it figure she'd be already talking? Kevin yelled, 'Let her go, we'll catch her,' and then the rear end of the car settled a little more. All of us who were watching made a collective sound, a spontaneous, terrified, 'Aaah,' because it looked like the three in the car might not get out; the car was going under and they'd be swept away.

I quit worrying about that when first Rosie and then the other two splashed into the river, and the water became a muddy froth full of bodies reaching, swimming, calling out, and pulling on lines; everybody was in the water but Gary and me. I was just about to put my weapon down so I could go and help, when in the slowly sinking open space at the rear of the Escalade two arms clad in vomit-yellow velour appeared, holding the long dark barrel and curving clip of an AK-47.

A squinting bewhiskered face sighted along the barrel, and I saw the man in the velour suit swing the weapon in a broad arc as he began firing bursts. Shots too fast to count spattered into the water and threw up sand along the shore. The mother of all bees stung the edge of my right foot and another one out of the same hive bit my left arm. I glanced down and saw blood running down my side. There was blood in the water too, and somebody yelling down there. Gary cried out when a bullet thunked into his vest, but he kept shooting and so did I, until the terrible man in the ugly suit dropped his weapon and plunged forward into the water.

He lay still there, bobbing in the confused churning eddies made by the many swimmers, until the current reasserted itself and he began to float away toward the Mississippi. Kevin, in the clear suddenly, saw him start to go. He said, 'Oh, no, you don't, you bastard,' and reached him in a couple of long-armed strokes. He seized a fistful of velour, dog-paddled left-handed till he could plant his own feet in the mud, and tugged him up on to the beach.

He stood over the muddy body gulping huge, ragged breaths of air for a few seconds before he bent and turned the man over. Then he straightened, met my eyes and smiled, made a circle of his thumb and forefinger, and said, 'Nice shot.'

I started to give him the same signal back but stopped, mesmerized by a row of bright-colored round blobs popping up along the edge of a low hill behind him. The blobs rose jerkily, like ducks in a shooting gallery, and faces began to appear below them. As they drew nearer, the faces began to wear expressions of extreme surprise and shock, rendered comical by the gleaming red and green helmets above them, and the Day-Glo orange, aqua and purple jackets below.

Attracted by the noise of our calamity, a crowd of kayakers had come up from their launching site just downstream. Their black neoprene splash-skirts hung above their bare knees and zippered booties like awkward tutus cut by an unskilled hand. When they saw the bloody man lying silent at the water's edge, they lined up on the brow of the hill and watched us in alarm, getting ready to flee like some new species of multi-colored wild game.

For a frozen minute, we all stared at each other in silence. It occurred to me that everybody in both groups was probably thinking, 'How soon will these people go away?'

TWELVE

'I can't believe,' the chief said Monday morning, 'that only two people died in that mess.'

'Two more unknown individuals,' I said, 'of apparent Russo-Serbian ethnicity, that nobody seems to be looking for.'

'Illegal aliens who caused untold pain and suffering the whole time they were here,' he said. 'I'm supposed to feel bad about them?'

'Nope. Legal or not, they pretty much got what they deserved, I guess.'

'But what?'

'I hate the fact that we still don't know who they were.'

'We will soon. We'll squeeze the locals till we find out.'

'I don't know. The gang they were working with in the Twin Cities – and the ones in Phoenix – had such an elaborate set-up, and now they all seem to be gone without trace.'

'What about the first man, the one they killed in the garage? Isn't BCA finding any matches for him?'

'Not so far,' I said. 'All we've got is the Mass card – for somebody who died somewhere in the Ukraine, that he must have cared about but was afraid to admit even knowing. How's that for a clue?'

'Outstanding. Before you ask for any more sympathy, can we talk about procedures?'

'Sure.' I sat back. Crossed my legs and straightened the crease in my pants. 'We broke up a drug ring, retrieved a great deal of stolen property, and rescued an experienced officer whose life was in danger. What don't you like?'

He shook his head sadly. 'See, before we even start to talk, you're on the defensive. Why can't you just listen a minute?'

'Because I know what you're going to say. We messed up a couple of vehicles that we don't have the money to replace, the chase was too long and too dangerous, we tore up city property and frightened a lot of innocent bystanders, and why the hell was my whole detective division out in it anyway?'

'Very good.' He almost smiled. 'Why were you all out there?'

'I've been over and over it in my mind. And I swear to you, Chief— Look, I know it doesn't sound like it's by the book, but if you take it one step at a time, at any point in the day we were only doing what we're supposed to do, and I don't see how we could have done it any other way.'

Frank has large, slightly protuberant blue eyes, and he fixed me now with that searching stare that over the years has elicited so much unwilling honesty. Forget waterboarding, sit in front of McCafferty's eyes for a while. I gazed back with utmost sincerity for a minute, and then recrossed my legs and said, 'Except that Rosie got out of the car after I told her not to.'

He nodded and waited. I said, 'But really, what would you do if you were in front of a store and heard "Officer needs assistance"? You'd go and try to help, right? So I really can't fault her for that.'

'What about letting herself get disarmed?'

'Now as to that, if you decide to hold a hearing on this, Gary will testify that she was ambushed. The bad guys were all talking on cell phones, the first two drivers warned the men in the Escalade about the officer shooting in front of the store, and, being total gorillas, that last pair must have decided to take her along for a bargaining chip if they got cornered. But Rosie was doing a good job of firing from cover until that guy jumped out from behind the truck and grabbed her. And Gary tried to go to her aid, though he was too far away. But after that, Chief, you'd have been proud if you'd seen how that kid performed, he was solid as a rock.'

'Uh-huh. You and Kevin both give the Krogstads way too much credit, just because they're baby-faced. Gary's been a cop six years, why shouldn't he know how to shoot?'

'He knows how to take a hit, too. He's got a crazy dent in his rib cage from where that bullet hit his vest. It damn near knocked him down, but he kept shooting.'

'I still don't understand how that Escalade driver could have been under water for so long and then come up shooting.'

'He wasn't. I'm pretty sure that what happened was the Escalade went into the water unevenly, so it was sitting higher on the driver's side. Rosie said he wasn't wearing a seat belt – doesn't that figure? – so as soon as the driver's air bag started to deflate he just floated up out of the water.'

'Yeah. New safety tip,' the chief said, rocking his big chair back, punishing the springs, 'don't wear your seat belt if you're going to drive your vehicle into large bodies of water.' He slammed some pens into a mug. 'Jesus! How the hell did he get the gun, though? What did you say it was?'

'An AK-47. Didn't it come in with the car?'

'No, it's gone. It must be in the river.'

'I suppose he had it in one of those luggage bins in the back. It's lucky he hadn't dug it out yet when Bo broke through that glass. He just hunkered down there, I guess, behind one of the seats, and bided his time. I think if he'd waited till we were all up on the shore he might have got into the water and floated away – we were all too damn wasted to follow him. But he decided to kill us all and take one of our cars.'

'I can't imagine why he thought he could do that.'

'Rosie said she saw his face when he first floated out of the water, and she thinks he was kind of irrational by then. She was talking a little bit loony herself for a while after we pulled her out of the water. She took a helluva beating rolling around in there during the chase.'

'I thought they had her tied up.'

'Yeah, her hands – to the headrest support on the back seat. You can imagine what it did to her shoulders.'

'She still in the hospital?'

'Getting out tomorrow, I think. In a body cast. Not exactly what she had in mind for a reunion with Bo—'

'Ah, that's on again, huh?'

'Well, you can't stay mad at a white knight

after he comes on his Harley and saves you from the villains.'

'He had no business being there at all.'

'I know. But he did do a helluva job, Chief. And Winnie – you ought to see the way that woman runs into a river. Jesus!'

'That right? Maybe we should have her teach the course, huh? Let's see, probably call it "How to Pass the Ten-Mile Trials We're Never Going to Run Again".'

'Yeah.' The conversation was turning ugly, so I hurried right along. 'Anyway, where was I? The bad-suit guy couldn't have been more than a few feet away when Bo reached in through that broken hole in the glass and opened the door. He must have ducked down behind a seat, I guess, Winnie said she never saw him – but of course she wasn't looking for anything but how to get Rosie out of there.'

'And the passenger? How did you know he was dead?'

'Rosie said he made one terrible noise, she looked around and saw he was impaled on a signpost.'

'The guys on the retrieval crew were seriously grossed out when they pulled that mess out of the river Saturday. But I said, "I'm not paying divers to go down and retrieve a body that's going to come up with

303

the car anyway – just get on with it".'

The chief sat back and sighed. 'He was quite a sight to behold, I admit.'

'You went out there?'

'I had to see it with my own eyes. I knew I was going to be taking heat about it for a long time, so I thought I better be sure of my facts.'

'Yeah, well.' I picked some lint off my jacket. 'You think you'd be taking any less heat if we let those bad guys drive away with Rosie Doyle in the car?'

'Oh, don't be ridiculous!' He slammed a number of items around on his desk. I sat still and watched the dust motes jump in a ray of afternoon sunshine. When he spoke again his voice was under tight control but not friendly at all. 'Of course we have to go to an officer's assistance when she requires it. But a dozen or so cars chasing a high-powered SUV for ten miles through the heart of town at speeds well beyond any expectation of safety? Not to mention goose parts and feathers flying around, a goddamn motorbike joining the chase for Christ's sake, and then a gun battle near a popular recreation area! We certainly have to ask some hard questions about the planning that led to all of that.'

One of the paper stacks he had smacked

304

into a pile slid off on to the floor. He took his time picking it up, and when he placed it neatly back on top of its pile the skin on his cheeks was dark red. 'I've scheduled the Critical Incident Debriefing for tomorrow night at seven, and I expect to see everybody there.' After a couple of seconds he vented a sigh that seemed to let the steam out of his anger and leave only sorrow behind. 'Everybody who's walking, that is. Vince Greeley won't be up and around for quite a while.'

'I know. He took a bad hit.'

'You seen him yet?'

'Yesterday. He couldn't talk much, he was in and out of the pain meds.'

'Dirty buggers ambushed him too, didn't they?

'Yeah. The armed robbery call was a fake.'

'What, they spotted the surveillance team?'

'I guess.' I wished we could leave it at that, but I knew tomorrow night's critical incident debriefing would surely reveal what Andy had learned from the pawnshop manager while he was bringing him in – that the bad-suit guys had spotted Rosie and Winnie during their tail Thursday night, and seen Rosie Friday morning during the ride-around I had so cleverly suggested. So now poor Vince, usually so cheery and talkative, was clinging silently to life at the end of an IV drip, and would be a long time getting his strength back. He took two slugs from a .357 Magnum – one in the iliac artery and one in the femoral – and would have bled to death on the floor of the pawnshop if either Hanenburger or the ambulance driver had been a few seconds slower.

No question, we had piled up a less than perfect score in skulking. But we were doing a lot better on straightforward investigation of the enablers who made the burglaries work so well. We saw digging the truth out of the locals as the best way to reclaim McCafferty's approval, so we were coming down hard on them.

'Half-crazy immigrants sneaking in from brutal places,' Frank said, 'have got to be stopped, but you can understand how they got that way. But supposedly respectable merchants who've lived here their whole lives and enjoyed all the good things we have, now they think it's cute to start robbing their neighbors? They're a disgrace.' It was all black and white for once, he said, no shades of gray here. 'Find everything you can pin on them, and I will personally see they get what they deserve.'

Which suited us fine, but we still had to figure out who did what.

'Let's get everybody together and divide

up the chores,' I said, and we held a meeting – like old times, people and property crimes together – at mid-morning around the big table in front of Ray's office. Not a very big meeting; if we were short-handed before, we were a skeleton crew now. The Krogstads had mustering-out chores to complete and a lot of paperwork for the uniforms and squads they'd be going back to, so we let them get on with that. We put the few who were never involved in the case, Clint Maddox and a couple of Kevin's investigators, in charge of answering all the calls that came in for the next two days. Kevin brought along Chris and Julie and two other detectives. Ray had Andy and Winnie.

'You want to go top down or bottom up on the locals?' Kevin said. 'Start with naughty boys or rotten papas?'

'I think we should start with the most insecure ones,' Julie Rider said.

'How do we know who that is?' Ray said.

'The two boys who were tied up in the back of the ABC Moving van,' Julie said. 'I bet they worked on their story all weekend.'

'Hey, that's right.' Kevin showed all his big white teeth in a delighted laugh. 'Arnie Aarsvold and Tony Knowles. They do have some "splainin" to do, don't they?'

I said, 'Are they out of the hospital yet?'

'They were never in,' Julie said. 'They said they weren't hurt, and the arresting officers had plenty to do, so ... they just unwrapped them and let them go.'

'You mean they're just ... out and about?'

'In school, I think,' Julie said, 'trying to look like good, studious boys.'

So that was how we played it – started with the boys and worked our way back to the dads. We didn't have far to go, because as soon as those two fathers heard their boys were being questioned by the police, they were downtown like a shot insisting we let them talk.

We made them wait until Tuesday. We wanted the boys' whole story on DVD first, two accounts obtained separately but surprisingly consistent. We made each father watch some of it, their firstborn sons explaining carefully which perfidies their fathers had taught them, and which they had added to the deal themselves, with the help of the crude immigrants who were so much smarter than they looked.

The boys had chosen to see the burglars as figures of fun – they called them 'the Slobovians'. The Slobovians had impenetrable accents, bad teeth, and terrible clothes – you could hardly take them seriously. They always struck when the houses were empty, so nobody ever got hurt. Well, Ricky Anderson, but he wasn't supposed to be there and he knew he had to keep his mouth shut if he wanted to protect his supply. So there was no real harm done. And for quite a while the deal had been terrific, bringing them more money, better dope, and the jazzy excitement of beating the system.

It had all turned to crap on them now. They wanted to reboot their lives, have their own clean rooms, easy Sundays, secure futures with the college admissions they had almost, but not quite, secured for themselves. 'All those years of making good grades,' Tony Knowles said, 'I guess that's all going to go away now, huh?'

They were so ready to deal.

It was especially bitter to them that the deal had gone sour on the very last day. They had been helping to load up the truck. 'That's what I figured,' Julie said. 'Two working boys, just like their daddies, always looking to make another buck.' She shook her glossy head. 'You could almost feel sorry for them, you know. They thought those thugs were just going to load up and wave goodbye.'

But when the heaviest items were stacked in the truck, they had turned toward the ramp to go in for the next load and found themselves facing five cold-eyed men with ropes and knives. Trussed up and gagged, they quickly noticed how their captors stashed them among the boxes as matter-of-factly as they might have put sheep there, to be slaughtered or kept alive depending on whether they had more need for meat or wool. Neither of the boys had ever encountered total indifference before – and it was, Arnie Aarsvold said, 'kind of a game-changer'. Of the two boys, he had come away from the experience with the most bounce left. He had plenty of regrets, but there was a corner of his personality that was already turning a small profit – having survived it, he was one step closer to manhood.

They had been wrapped up in burlap and tied like rolls of carpet, but somehow when the police boarded the van they had managed to move enough to attract attention. 'The guys who made the traffic stop told me,' Arnie said, already embroidering the tale a little, 'they almost shit purple when the carpet started to move.'

The horror still clung to Tony Knowles. He grew pale and ghostlike as he told his story – part of him was still a hostage. The screaming chase across town in the van had hardly registered with him. 'From the minute they grabbed us,' he said, just above a whisper, 'I could see that at some point we were going to die.' It was absolutely clear to him that the Rutherford Police Department had handed him back his life. The danger still ahead for him, I thought, was that he wasn't sure he wanted it back.

It was that realization that broke David Knowles. He had been all bluster and bluff when we started, full of statements that began 'I won't be treated like a criminal' or 'I don't think you realize who you're talking to'. But when he saw how damaged his son was, he put his big veined hands over his face and sat with his shoulders heaving, tears running out between his fingers.

'I got them into it,' he said, when he could talk. 'God forgive me, I told them what we wanted done and what they would earn for doing it. The times you were asking me about, when the records showed they were working both places? They were always working for me those times.

'I already had most of the information about when people would be out. I just needed them to go in with their little cleaning carts and figure the best ways in and out. I showed them how to jimmy some locks, open some windows, make a diagram with two or three alternatives. And I got them to find out how much of a bribe Arnie's little

311

brother would take to shut up about them skipping out on their hours at the nursery. I turned them all into perfect little crooks.'

Kevin had been unusually gentle in that interview, giving Knowles all the time he needed. But now as I watched the monitor I saw him glance at his watch, then pull himself up and look down his handsome nose at David Knowles, who is a large, plain man with no memorable features.

'Why'd you do it?' he asked sharply. 'Are you going broke?'

'No!' Improbably, David Knowles went back to acting insulted. 'We have a fine clientele, we've always made a good living.'

Kevin stared at him silently, blinking, and Knowles seemed to deflate slowly, like a balloon with a pinhole. 'It was just ... a chance for some extras, for once,' he said. 'I've always been a drudge. Other people win prizes, have a run of luck, inherit money, get by on their looks. I just go slogging along. These men came to me and ... I thought, let's have some extras for once, about damn time.' Then he was weeping unashamedly, with great racking sobs that shook the table. 'And now I've wrecked my son's life!'

So the chief was wrong, it was not all black and white, any more than it ever is. It was all shades of tiresome and wearying gray that

312

took weeks to sort out and left everybody poorer and sadder. If there was any upside, I think it was that two high-school seniors got disabused of the notion that they could have it both ways – but they paid a very high price for that lesson.

'Was that the hardest part?' Trudy asked me, one of the several times I described some more aspects of the case to her. 'When Dave Knowles cried?'

'Just about,' I said. 'Although – this is crazy, but do you want to know the very worst moment in the whole mess?'

'I guess,' she said. 'This won't make me throw up, will it?'

'No, it's not like that. But that Friday when the whole thing blew up – the day of the chase – and we went through all that craziness and had to wait for the ambulance for Rosie and Ruskie—'

'Ruskie needed an ambulance, too?'

'He got shot in the arm, too, while he was in the water. It wasn't bad – through and through on his upper arm, but it bled like crazy, so they hooked him up to an IV. And they bandaged me up, my foot and my arm, right out there at the river, and Bo got treated for his glass cuts ... It seemed like we were there for hours, and then we had to figure out how to get all the cars back. And when

313

we got back to the station, you know what? It was only two in the afternoon! We still had three hours to work.'

'And that really bothered you more than the chase or the shooting, or the crazy scene with the kayakers? The three quiet hours in Government Center that came after?'

'We all had a case of the jerks, you know? I couldn't work, and I couldn't sit still. Too much had happened. A couple of times I thought my watch had stopped. And I kept thinking, Christ, even when that filthy clock finally gets around to showing five I have to go over there and get Ben. And if that kid screams all the way home, I really don't think I can stand it.'

'Ah,' she said. 'So that was the day...'

'Yup. I said to Maxine, "Trudy told me once that she left a little device here for some day when I felt like I needed some silence." And she said, "I thought I heard a lot of sirens around town today." And she went and got the pacifier out of the drawer.'

'It worked, too, didn't it?'

'It works every time. He loves it devotedly.' I looked at him, asleep in his downstairs crib. His color is about halfway between my toasted almond and Trudy's Minnesota blond, and when he is sleeping he gets a little paler and looks more angelic. I touched his cheek,

314

just barely, and he wrinkled his nose. 'Good intentions are so easy to lose, and so hard to get back.'

'Good intentions? He's a baby, for God's sake!'

'I meant mine. He has a new little light in his eye, now, when I strap him into the seat for the ride home. I can see him thinking, "I'll give you about thirty seconds to come up with that sucker thing, before I start to yell."'

She laughed. 'Don't be too hard on him. We're all pretty good at this wanting stuff.' She hung her dishtowel around my neck and drew me closer. 'It's not all bad. After all, wanting got us where we are today.'

'You're right,' I said. 'Let's not worry about it, let's want some more.'